RIVER BOUND

A SYDNEY BRENNAN NOVELLA

JUDY K. WALKER

TITLES BY JUDY K. WALKER

THE SYDNEY BRENNAN MYSTERIES
(IN ORDER OF PUBLICATION)
Back to Lazarus (A Sydney Brennan Novel)
Secrets in Stockbridge (A Sydney Brennan Novella)
The Perils of Panacea (A Sydney Brennan Novel)
No Safe Winterport (A Sydney Brennan Novella)
Braving the Boneyard (A Sydney Brennan Novel)
River Bound (A Sydney Brennan Novella)

THE DEAD HOLLOW TRILOGY
Prodigal
Founder

Cover design by Robin Ludwig Design Inc.
http://www.gobookcoverdesign.com/

ISBN: 978-1-946720-05-4

Thanks as always to my beloved Epiphanator, without whom none of this would be possible

Author's Note on Time:
This story take place in early 2005, after the events of Braving the
Boneyard.

1

Is it bad luck to get held at gunpoint on a first date?

Allow me to rephrase. Whatever the reason—luck, fate, karma, because you just knocked off a liquor store —any time you're being held at gunpoint isn't exactly a banner day. But if that day also happens to be your first date with someone, is that a sign? An omen of ill tidings for your budding relationship? That is, assuming you live through the date.

I'd had less than twenty-four hours to cultivate misgivings about this particular outing, but they'd been tickling at the back of my brain ever since I'd gotten the invitation. It had been an evening of unexpected phone calls. First, my friend Noel Thomas—not exactly a barfly—had called to invite me for a drink after work. Then my sister checked in with her latest pregnancy news. I suppose I shouldn't be surprised by her calls—now I hear from her every week or so—but after more than a decade without contact, I still hadn't gotten used to seeing her number appear on my phone. Last night, I'd had the unique pleasure of listening to Lisa dance around, searching for an acceptable word for her latest symptom: flatulence. *Fart* was out; believe it or not, *toot* won the day. She also had an itchy belly. Exciting stuff.

Shadows had fallen around downtown Tallahassee by the time Lisa finished cataloging her symptoms. (To be fair, no matter how strange or uncomfortable the bodily transformation, she was too thrilled to finally be pregnant to ever actually complain). I locked up my office and sat on the cool, concrete front steps, pulling my thin cardigan close. I could distinguish the shape of the buds on the sweetgum tree that arced over the house-turned-office building, but not their pale green color. Echoes of music drifted down from nearby Kleman Plaza, and from the other direction came a vague hum of people and traffic and the glow of lights. Friday night in the Big City.

"Why am I still here?" I asked aloud.

When the only other mammal in earshot, a squirrel perched on a branch above me, couldn't give me a reasonable answer, I stopped stalling and hopped in my little Cabrio. Traffic was light, and Cecil's tires crackled in the gravel parking lot of Cooper's Bar in just over fifteen minutes, making me only slightly late. I climbed the steps and crossed the raised threshold carefully. Although a semi-regular at Cooper's, getting through the front door without tripping was always a challenge.

Noel sat on a stool at the bar and swiveled toward me as I approached. Her straightened hair was pulled tight against her skull, and she was in weekday banker mode: gray pantsuit with matching pumps, a blouse some shade of orange that popped against her dark skin but would make me look like the risen dead, and a sweating glass of something iced and clear that probably was not water.

"You're still wearing those cowboy boots?" she asked.

I hadn't seen Noel since I'd taken her on an ill-fated surveillance gig with me a couple of weeks ago, wearing said boots. I tugged at my jeans as I sat, stretching one leg long to admire my brown leather footwear.

"It's Florida. I've got to wear them while my feet won't sweat. Besides, I seem to remember you wearing cowboy boots the last time I saw you." I glanced around furtively, adding in a stage whisper, "And you're black."

She ignored my intentionally provocative remark and protested, "That was to a bar."

The owner of Cooper's popped his graying head out from the back and smiled when he saw me. "The usual?" Glenn called out.

I gave him a thumbs-up, then inclined my head toward the rows of bottles a few feet away and asked Noel, "Is this not a bar?"

She rolled her eyes. "You wore those to work today, too."

I shrugged. With my office so close to the capitol, I'd seen legislators wear boots to work—who cared about a lowly private investigator? Glenn set my Abita Amber and an icy glass on the bar. He raised his own corrected Coke, bumped my glass, then popped a few wasabi peas into his mouth from a bulk bag. One bounced off his mustache. I leaned over the bar to watch its progress and was also treated to a view of Glenn's feet. "He's wearing cowboy boots to work, too."

"Your friend here denies she had a shitty week, but I don't believe her," Glenn said, tossing the errant pea in the trash and his long, reddish-brown braid over his shoulder.

I gestured toward the far end of the bar for more privacy. Noel rose with her half-full drink.

"Don't worry," I told Glenn, grabbing a handful of wasabi peas. "I brought a rubber hose."

One of Glenn's caterpillar brows rose, as though it had seen a particularly delectable leaf. I followed on Noel's heels, but Glenn's warm chuckle at my back made me shiver. My beer sloshed precipitously, a frothy film crawling out of the glass to coat my hand.

I slid onto a stool as Noel said in a low voice, "You're chummy with the bartender."

"Owner," I said, trying to figure out how to wipe the spilled beer from one hand while the other hand still held wasabi peas. Impossible, so I tossed them all into my mouth, crunched a few times and told Noel, "And tonight isn't about me. We're here to talk about what's going on with you."

"What do you mean?" Noel's face went still. The woman excelled at impassive.

"You're drinking vodka—"

"Gin," she corrected.

My face wrinkled in disgust. I hate gin. "Even worse. A couple of weeks ago, you were drinking Long Island Iced Teas like they were..."

"Iced tea?" she suggested, lip curling in an almost smile.

"You're not usually such a smartass. Of course, I'd venture to say it's out of character for you to have someone hold your hair while you puke in a parking lot like a college student, too."

My phone rang, and I pulled it free from my purse for the final unexpected call of the evening. Speak of the devil—it was Mike Montgomery, an investigator who lived closer to the Panhandle's Redneck Riviera than to the capital, and the man who'd been kind enough to hold Noel's hair. I silenced the phone.

Noel stared down at the bar, and I worried my previous comment had pushed her too far. "I'm not judging; I'm just observing. You're not yourself lately."

I expected Noel to challenge me, to become defensive, but when she lifted her head she seemed relieved. "I've been seeing someone."

"Okay," I said, waiting for a boot of a different kind to drop.

"He's married," she admitted.

I couldn't keep the surprise from my face. That's not true; I probably could have, but couldn't think of any good reason why I should.

"I know," she acknowledged. "But I just told him it's over."

Last year, Noel had learned some ugly truths about her mother's life and death. And although she didn't talk about it, I knew she'd struggled to come to terms with what that meant for her own feminine identity. Her grandmother had also raised her with rigid ideas of right and wrong, and I was pretty sure she put adultery in the latter camp. Whatever Noel and the married man had shared must have been more than physical, and it must be costing her now to have ended it.

"I'm sorry," I said.

She nodded, bit her lip, then said in a firm voice, "I did the right thing."

"Doesn't mean it was easy. How's he taking it?"

Her brows pinched together, making her appear more confused than anything else. "He wasn't happy, but he agreed it was the right thing to do. We both know we wouldn't be good together long-term, and he doesn't want to leave his wife."

"Of course not," I said. "He wants it both ways."

She glared at me, and I apologized. Over my shoulder, two men playing pool (early thirties, clean-shaven in jeans and long-sleeved shirts) racked for a new game. I squeezed my glass to hide my flinch against the loud clacking as one of them broke, then took another sip of beer and wished I'd gone for something darker. Or stronger.

"So you want to do something tomorrow, take your mind off it?" I asked.

"Thanks, but I can't. Family obligations." She smiled. "You're welcome to come with me. I'm sure Grandma Harrison would love to see you."

I happen to know the woman hates my guts. "Noel, sarcasm does not suit you, but I appreciate the effort. Want to see if Glenn can scrounge up something more substantial than wasabi peas?"

"For you, I'll bet he will."

"It's not like that," I said.

"Hey," she protested, holding up her hands. "I'm not judging; just observing."

I shook my head, but the creeping corner of my mouth betrayed me. "Okay, I had that coming," I admitted, then leaned in. "It only happened once. Last year. And there were extenuating circumstances."

Like we'd just almost been killed. Neither of us had made a move to repeat it. But we'd certainly enjoyed each other's company that night, and the man had always relished the occasional jab of innuendo.

"Of course there were," Noel said. "You're a closet adrenaline junkie with a weakness for bad boys. The badder the better."

My mouth fell open. But she wasn't wrong.

"Sorry," she said, and made a zipping motion across her lips. "You said tonight is about *my* bad choices, not yours. What do we need for that, a three-day weekend? A week-long retreat?"

It was worth the insult to hear her laugh. And honestly, her timeframe probably gave me too much credit in the common sense department.

I waved at Glenn, brought my hands together in prayer, and topped it off with my best hungry puppy dog eyes. The man could put together some mean bar grub when he wanted to; the challenge was making him want to. He'd started his grumbling way toward the fridges when my cell phone buzzed again. This time I answered.

"Mikey!" I said, with the exuberance of the old Life cereal commercial.

"Sydney!" he said, echoing my tone. "What are you doing tomorrow?"

Noel raised an eyebrow provocatively, so I turned my back to her.

"Not a thing," I said.

"Want to go canoeing with me?"

"You mean, in a canoe?" I asked. Had I ever been in a canoe? I'd been in a kayak, and it was not the most comfortable mode of transport. "On a river?"

"Yes," he said slowly, as though wondering if I was cracking up. "They tend to work better that way. I didn't wake you up, did I?"

Noel's eyes burned a hole in my back and confused thoughts ricocheted around my skull. "So is this, like, a date?"

Did I imagine the pause on the other end?

"Yes," he answered. "The fun kind. Not the am-I-dressed-appropriately and is-this-a-shitty-restaurant kind. Are you in?"

Mike was someone I relied upon a lot—even when I didn't reach out to him, I felt better knowing that I could. His friendship had been one of the best things to come out of the past year's challenges. At some point (it snuck up on me, so I'm not sure when), I'd realized I wanted more than friendship. He hadn't seemed ready to give it. Now that he was... I knew I should be happy, but I was scared.

"Syd? You still there?" he asked.

Scared... In the past year, I'd been kidnapped. I'd been beaten. I hadn't been shot, but not for lack of trying. I'd been threatened, and more than once, I'd thought I was going to die. And this *scared* me? Bullshit. I wasn't scared. I was stupid. And once you recognized it, there was no excuse for being stupid.

"Sure," I said. "Why not?"

"You'll have to meet me early—say seven-thirty—at a place near Marianna."

Ouch—that was why not. Mike gave me directions to a small shopping center right off Interstate 10, about an hour-and-a-half drive from my house. Did I mention at seven-thirty on a Saturday morning? He must have felt my hesitation.

"All you have to do is show up. I'll supply lunch," he said. "And remember, it'll be seven-thirty Central Time."

Which gave me an extra hour coming from the Eastern time zone and meant I didn't have to leave until seven. "Okay. I can do that," I said. "But I have to be home at a reasonable time. I have a brunch meeting Sunday morning."

Glenn arrived with a mouth-watering bowl of chunky, spicy queso as I hung up. His stirring spoon still rested in the ceramic crock. I pulled it free for a decadent mouthful while Glenn dumped tortilla chips into another bowl. He swatted my hand, and the spoon rattled against my teeth.

"Were you raised by wolves?" asked the man who used to ride motorcycles with some of the scariest men in the South. He took the spoon from me gingerly in two fingers and tossed it in the sink.

"How does one dress appropriately for canoeing?" I asked.

"A canoeing *date*," added Noel, who'd obviously been eavesdropping.

Glenn looked at me and snorted. "You ever been canoeing?"

"No."

"Dress to get wet. And take something dry for after.

You're gonna freeze your ass off." He inclined his head toward Noel and added, "Come to think of it, that's not a bad strategy for a date."

"You mean, the clothes-changing requirement? Or because she'll need someone to warm her up after?" Noel smirked.

I blushed and restrained my twitchy middle finger. Well, almost.

2

I left Cooper's at a reasonable hour, but still didn't get enough sleep that night. Meeting Mike on time the next morning required a monster go-cup of coffee—the kind that barely fit in the cupholder—and intermittent, steering wheel-squeezing pep talks *(you're not really that tired —suck it up)*. Mike was easy to spot, his head (clad in baseball cap and sunglasses) popping out of his yellow Jeep in an otherwise empty mall parking lot. He wore a faded maroon, long-sleeved T-shirt over dark, crinkly pants that looked like they belonged in a pick-up basketball game. Or maybe all pants look like basketball pants when you're Mike's height.

I was dressed similarly, except in the kind of snug, synthetic leggings people who actually run might wear while running. (I had no idea how they'd come into *my* possession, but was counting on them drying quickly.) I couldn't help feeling my wardrobe suggested I was recovering from a hangover (not actually the case—I'd stuck to a single beer with Noel). Mike, on the other hand, appeared to be casually dressed because he was all kinds of energetic and ready to do shit. Like canoeing. I grabbed my bag from Cecil's trunk and locked up.

Mike smiled as he opened the passenger door for me. "Good morning, sunshine."

Mike has a very nice smile that I couldn't help mirroring. However, I'd once used that phrase (with additional, more colorful language) to greet a seriously annoyed attorney when the three of us were working a case together. "I look that good, huh?" I asked, tossing my bag behind the seat. "How is Richard?"

"He's fine. But no shop talk today," Mike said.

He smiled—yes, *again*, and it occurred to me I could get used to seeing that first thing in the morning—before handing me a small paper bag. Something warm and moist was beginning to seep through. I peeked in and pulled a pile of napkins from atop my prize, a fresh (did I mention still-warm?) glazed donut.

"Ohh, thank you," I moaned.

"Thank you for meeting me at such an ungodly hour."

Lost in contemplating the sugar, I missed what Mike said as he pulled onto the highway. A moment later, his hand patted my seat belt in a gentle reminder, and I buckled up with sticky fingers. Beneath its glaze, the donut's thin, firm skin held in soft and gooey carbohydrate heaven. I could get used to this, too. Except then I'd have to wear stretchy pants every day.

I sighed and wiped my hands on about seven napkins, then glanced over my shoulder between the seats.

"Don't worry," Mike said. "There's more food stashed in the back. Lunch, even."

I gave his arm a smack. "Smartass. I was looking for clues to our destination. I don't see a canoe anywhere."

"I used to own one," Mike said, wistful. "Had to get rid of it when I moved. But a friend of mine runs an outfitter near here. He'll hook us up. This river's a popular spot for canoeing and kayaking—"

"In February?" I asked.

He had the good grace to blush. "No, but that means we'll have it all to ourselves. And it's almost March. You have a jacket, right?"

"Yeah, in my bag."

"We probably won't need it. The weather's supposed to be nice. I was saying, my buddy'll drop us off. We'll paddle down-river for a few hours—take our time, stop when we feel like it —and he'll pick us up at the end. Super simple, low stress."

"All right," I said. "I'll remember that when an alligator jumps in our canoe looking for a ride."

"This time of year, I doubt you have to worry too much about gator acrobatics," he said. "They'll be content to bask in the sun."

"That makes two of us." Except I didn't even wait for the sun, slipping my sunglasses into my shirt pocket and pulling my Red Sox cap low over my eyes. Sugar rush or not, *date* or not, the thin sleep and early morning start were catching up with me.

I'd almost dozed off when I felt the Jeep's engine slow and reluctantly opened my eyes. The highway seemed deserted, desolate even, raised a foot or so above the surrounding land-scape. The pavement was edged by pale, sandy dirt, with a few inches of brown grass between it and the guardrail. Then there wasn't much more real estate between the guardrail and the drop-off to the river. On the opposite side of the road, bleached deciduous tree trunks stood like gray bones among the dull green palmettos, live oaks, and scattered pines.

The sun had burned the early overcast away, and Mike squinted at the road. "I know the turn is somewhere close."

"Shouldn't you be wearing your glasses?" I asked. It was rare to see him without them.

"Haven't we done this conversation before?"

I thought back to a lovely evening last year when we'd gone sailing on the Gulf. Before identifying a dead body. "You and boats and glasses don't mix. But I can help you with street signs."

"Probably a good idea," he admitted, pulling a pair of sunglasses from his cupholder and slipping them on.

"What are we looking for?" I asked.

"There!" He pointed at a sign ahead of us on the right, half hidden by the overgrown roadside brush.

I blinked, certain I'd misread it. "Seriously—this place is called Shark's?"

"Sharkey's," Mike corrected.

He was right; as we made the turn, the second syllable and bottom line on the sign became visible: *Sharkey's Canoe Shack.*

"Tell me this guy isn't some kind of Jimmy Buffett wannabe."

"Hardly," Mike replied. "Sharkey is his last name."

The outfitter's driveway dropped from the highway more suddenly than I'd expected. My stomach lurched with the Jeep, and the cloud of dust trailing our tires would have made a road warrior proud.

"Sorry about that," Mike said, but he was grinning, with teeth showing and everything.

We crossed a parking lot with an identity crisis (shell or gravel or cement? how about all three). The main building was a simple, one-story wooden structure, separated from a river the color of milky tea by a long, plank dock. A smaller structure looked like the illegitimate offspring of a canoe rack and a chicken coop, storing a couple dozen stacked canoes with some pretense of security.

I didn't see anyone outside, and the only other vehicles in the parking lot were two small, nondescript cars, and a van with the same yellow and blue logo that hung above the entrance to the building. Mike pulled in alongside one of the cars. "Shall we?" he asked.

The exterior of the building had bleached gray, but the interior was surprisingly clean, with bright wood paneling. Racks of tourist brochures stood near the entrance. A couple of plastic kayaks were stacked along the wall to the right, along with a single canoe a little too close to foot traffic for my tastes. On the left side, the wall protruded to accommodate restrooms and an employees-only area. The space between the doors was covered with framed photos of people, customers and staff—some wet, some dry, some posed, some spontaneous, but almost all of them laughing.

"Hello?" Mike called. "Levi?"

We kept walking, and at around the room's midpoint, the space broadened again on the left side, creating an alcove with T-shirts, a display of local books, and stuffed alligators and manatees. The checkout counter was directly ahead, with more shelves of T-shirts and water bottles, sunscreen, and protein bars. To the right of the counter was a broad picture window with a nice view of the river, but we didn't see anyone outside.

"Good morning," a man hailed from behind us. I recognized him from one of the posed photos. Late twenties with dark hair, wearing a T-shirt with the outfitter's logo stretching just the right amount across his biceps, he strode confidently across the space.

"I'm Ken," he said, raising his hand as he approached. "You must be Mike. Sharkey wanted me to tell you he's sorry —he had to step out for a while—but he should be back by the time you folks finish, if you can stick around to catch up then."

Mike's head dipped in acknowledgment. "I'm sure I'll need some recovery time before I can lift my arms to drive home. This is my friend, Sydney."

"Does that mean you'll be carrying him back?" Ken asked, shaking my hand.

"Can you seriously see that happening?" I asked. At six feet, two inches, Mike was nearly a foot taller than me; thrown over my shoulder, his legs would probably drag the ground.

"I try not to make assumptions," Ken said, pulling forward a lanky young man that I hadn't noticed standing behind him. "This is my cousin, Leonard. He's helping out on the weekends and this summer before he heads off to college."

Leonard nodded awkwardly, removing his hands from his jean pockets just long enough to tuck his stringy, blond hair behind an ear. "I'll make sure everything's secure," he said, and brushed past me and out the front door.

"Okay," Ken said, clapping his hands together. "Last chance to hit the head, and then bring your stuff over to the van."

My mother and I hadn't agreed on much, but if there's one thing she'd drilled into my head, it was to take advantage of restroom facilities while you have them. Mike, being of the easy peeing gender, said he'd meet me at the car. I lingered in the restroom, trying to decide whether to fill my pockets with toilet paper since I hadn't thought to bring any. That is, until I realized my leggings didn't have any pockets. Preparation was overrated.

Pushing the door open with my butt, I heard Ken's voice coming from around the corner in the alcove. "What did he say when he left?"

"I told you—"

"No," Ken cut off his younger cousin, "I mean, what were his exact words?"

"I don't know," Leonard said, his voice rising in pitch.

"Just that he had something to take care of and he'd be back by lunch."

"There's something you're not telling me," Ken said. "And if I find out it's got something to do with—"

He stopped abruptly as Mike entered through the front door, eyes scanning the space. Mike's face relaxed when he caught sight of me.

"Did you think I slipped out the back?" I joked, following him outside to his Jeep.

"It had occurred to me," he said, hands on hips, staring at the vehicle. "I'm trying to decide whether to take my cell phone."

"I'm leaving mine," I said. I'm not exactly religious about keeping it close, even when there aren't water hazards, and it's not like I had anyone who would freak out if I didn't answer right away. "Are you expecting any calls?"

"Possibly Richard, about a case we've got coming up," Mike said, then locked up his side and came around to mine. He reached past me to put his phone in the glovebox. "Which is reason enough to leave it behind. No shop talk."

I took off my baseball cap and shoved my fingers in my curls, battling toward the ends to form a loose ponytail. "I think I like this decisive Mr. Montgomery, Weekend Edition."

"Really?" he asked, stepping into my space.

My face burned as I shoved my hair through the back opening of my cap. Mike's hands hovered, and I thought they'd settle on my hips. Instead, he reached toward my hat and tucked in a stray curl. I shivered involuntarily as his fingertip brushed my neck. This time, he was the one who blushed, and I was mildly disappointed when he stepped back. I snagged my jacket and coffee dregs while he grabbed a cooler bag from behind the seats, but couldn't imagine needing anything else.

"I hope you put on sunscreen," he said.

I adjusted the collar on my button-down shirt. Had I put on "real" sunscreen? I use an SPF moisturizer every day, just to travel the short distance from one interior space to another in the Sunshine State. But heading outdoors requires a whole other level of preparation. With my red hair and pale skin, people stand clear of me at beaches, afraid to be caught in the flame zone when I spontaneously combust.

"So how long have you known this Sharkey guy?" I asked.

"Six years, maybe? No, at least seven. Why?" Mike slid the bag over his arm and adjusted his sunglasses and hat, a faded blue beater advertising a local seafood shack.

Oh yeah—that's why I was squinting. I pulled my own sunglasses from my pocket. "Does he run a pretty tight ship?"

"Are we back on the Parrothead thing? Or are you afraid our boat will sink?" Mike asked.

"No, it's just—" Ken and his cousin waited ahead of us at the van, Ken all smiles. I linked my elbow through Mike's, and he paused just long enough for me to say, "Sharkey didn't actually tell Ken he wouldn't be here. It's probably nothing."

"Huh," Mike said.

We kept walking, arm in arm. Ken opened the van door for us, and its grinding, metallic slide was loud in the empty lot.

"I need to keep an eye on things here, so Leonard is driving you guys to the launch. Sharkey and I will see you back here this afternoon." Ken slid the door shut and gave it a smack, then yelled through the closed window, "Have fun!"

The van's engine was already running, and Leonard rounded over the steering wheel, white-knuckling it. I fastened my seat belt and bit my lip against asking how long he'd had his driver's license. At least it was only the van; they'd strapped the single canoe to its roof rather than hooking up the trailer. Mike lowered his sunglasses and looked at me with wide eyes, mock terrified. I swatted his arm and smiled. At least until the van lurched so dramatically from the steep driveway to the state road that my teeth snapped together and Mike grunted.

When it seemed the van was on a stable path down the highway, Mike pulled enough slack into his belt to lean in and ask, "So, Leonard, where you going to school in the fall?"

"Huh?" the young man asked, looking up at the rearview mirror. One clenched hand released the wheel just long enough to point at his ears. "Sorry—I can't hear you up here."

Mike nodded and raised his hands to signal, *No worries*.

At least that meant there was no small talk pressure. The window on my side had some kind of film over it that made the world blurry and me carsick if I looked at it too long. I ignored the passing scenery and curled up against Mike instead. He slipped his arm around me and I closed my eyes.

This time, I was fully asleep when the slowing engine roused me. I looked up to find Leonard pulling across a lane through a gap in traffic I wouldn't have attempted in my Cabrio, much less in a van. Mike squeezed my forearm in alarm, but we both held our tongues.

I'm not sure who was more relieved—Mike and I, or Leonard—when the teenager switched off the ignition. We were parked in a dirt lot, maybe twenty-five yards from the river. It was broader here than it had been at Sharkey's, and the color was closer to blue than brown. I admired it—the swirls, the ripples, the sense of playfulness—while the two men got the canoe down from the top of the van. (I didn't see a step stool, so I didn't bother to offer assistance.)

"You need me to help you get it to the water?" Leonard asked.

"No," I said, grabbing a loop on one end. A pair of life vests lay inside. "I think we've got it."

"Cool," the teenager said, hurrying back to the van.

"Leonard!" Mike called out. "How about some paddles?"

Leonard goggled at us. "They're not in there?"

Mike told him they weren't, but Leonard raced over and looked in the hull anyway. "Oh, jeez," he said, picking at his lip. "I can't believe... wait, we usually keep a couple of spares in the van."

The young man opened the back of the van and nearly sank to the ground in relief. "These aren't the best paddles," he said, tugging them free of the seat supports.

"But they'll do the job," Mike affirmed, taking them from him. "Thanks, Leonard."

Leonard nodded, and kept nodding all the way back to the van. Mike settled the paddles in the canoe's hull, and we watched the cloud of dust as Leonard sped away.

"Be glad you fell asleep," Mike said. "I spent the past twenty minutes with a deep and abiding awareness of the fragility of life."

I laughed. "You must be getting old."

"Old enough to be glad that for the rest of the day, we'll have nothing but alligators to prompt any serious contemplations of mortality."

"Amen to that," I said, picking up my end of the canoe, blissfully unaware of what the day had in store.

3

"This really was a fantastic idea," I said. For only about the third time. "Thank you."

"Again, you're very welcome," Mike said from the stern. "But how about a little less sightseeing and a little more helping out up there?"

I turned and reminded him, "You just told me to stop splashing you and whacking your paddle. You know, you can't have it both ways."

The soft slur of our paddles—okay, mostly Mike's paddle —cutting through the smooth water, and of the canoe gliding atop it, was just about the sweetest thing I'd ever heard. And at the moment it was one of the only sounds, with most of the insects dormant. A few birds repeated the same whistling call, something like you'd hear from a coach on a sports field trying to get a lagging player's attention. Occasionally, a car droned in the distance, but the highway never cut close enough, nor was it traveled enough, to be intrusive.

With that in mind, I gazed at the old bridge that spanned the river ahead of us and wondered how many years it had been since it had carried cars. It looked as though a fat squirrel would be enough to bring it down now. And yet, the twelve-year-old in me did dearly want to climb its girders. Or stare up at it... I glanced back at Mike again, grinning, and saw the same thought cross his face.

"I can't do it, but you probably can," he said, sliding off his seat to kneel in front of it. "Just don't capsize us."

I scooted backward until I sat on a life vest.

"Watch the yoke," Mike said.

The back of my head struck a wooden crossbar as I tried to lie down. So that's what a yoke was. My neck twinged as I twisted my head to get beneath it. Once I'd settled, about eight inches separated my face from the yoke, triggering the tickling fingers of claustrophobia. I pushed that—and the desire to yank my synthetic leggings out of my butt—from my mind, raising my knees and resting my feet on the bow seat.

"Comfy?" Mike asked.

I tilted my head and found myself staring at his knees, positioned on the other life vest, and at the crotch of his thankfully baggy pants. "Not really," I admitted.

But it was worth it. The current was slow and gentle and the shore sandy, so there was little danger of us running aground, whether I was helping or not. The sky overhead was overcast but bluish, with pale clouds piled like discarded laundry and strands stretched between like chewing gum. Floating beneath the bridge, the air seemed to reverberate, and I imagined I could hear echoes of traffic long past. Rusty metal beams appeared both ready to fall upon us, and destined to be sentinels in some future dystopian world that had left us behind. My inclination was toward the latter when I sat up to see an alligator staring warily from the branch of a fallen, submerged tree. Its eyes upon us made my scalp prickle with excitement, and it was small enough—maybe four feet—that I had a powerful compulsion to touch it, to feel the hard ridges of its skin and explore the space between them with my bare fingers.

"Easy there, Steve Irwin," Mike called from the stern as I bent over the side of the canoe. "You're lucky to see him this early."

I grinned as I settled back in my seat. "We had alligators in central Florida, too, but they seemed different near urban areas."

"Like pigeons with big teeth?"

I laughed. "Exactly."

Mike felt compelled to demonstrate a few steering strokes —in case he broke an arm and I had to paddle us back to civilization—but they didn't come naturally to me. It didn't help that I was stubbornly resistant to the alphabet naming system. ("It's only a J stroke if you do it on the left side," I insisted.) I was also stubbornly resistant to doing anything that felt like work or decision-making or thinking in general on this unusual day off. And—oh, yeah—on a first date.

The river carried us beneath another highway bridge, this one still functioning, to a launch site that was slightly more developed than the one where Leonard had dropped us off. The edge of a paved parking lot was visible before it swung around out of sight behind scraggly brush and palmettos. I caught the flash of a faded green portable toilet on the far side as we passed by.

"Did you need to stop?" Mike asked.

What a lovely thought—it probably hadn't been emptied since last summer. I flicked my paddle, baptizing his knee with cold river water. "I think I'm finally getting the hang of this."

"You think?" Mike asked, voice playful. He dipped his paddle into the water, gave a quick pull and a twist, and suddenly my cheeks were wet, just a few tablespoons of water that ran down my nose to drip off the end.

"How did you do that?" I asked, dumbfounded.

He raised a brow and held back a smile, trying to look mysterious. "Skills acquired in a past life."

"Really?" I asked, dubious.

My travel cup of coffee was wedged in the narrow space at the front, secured by my balled-up jacket. I pulled the cup free, gave it a quick rinse and filled it with river water. My wrist sagged under the weight of twenty ounces of tannic liquid.

"You wouldn't," Mike said, but the look on his face confirmed he absolutely knew I would. "You sure you want to go down that road?"

My wrist flick was less graceful than Mike's had been, but it got the job done. I did, however, wimp out at the last moment and adjust downward, soaking his chest rather than his face. The excess water from my go-cup trickled down my hand to my wrist, and I was shocked by its chill.

"Now you started something," Mike said, grinning mischievously.

He stowed his paddle in the hull and began slowly crawling toward me. The canoe rocked gently, and he grabbed the gunwales on both sides to steady it as he stepped over the yoke. The bow sank noticeably deeper in the water without quite torpedoing as he crept closer.

"Oh no, you don't," I said, an edge of desperation in my voice. I did not want to be dumped in the freezing water. Unable to retreat, I hopped my seat and closed the distance between us instead. We faced each other, just a few inches separating us, Mike sitting on his feet and me gripping the gunwales to maintain my balance on my knees. I still had to look up at him, and when I spoke again it felt as though I'd forgotten to breathe.

"Are *you* sure you want to go down that road?" I asked.

It was hard to read his expression, in his sunglasses and

cap, but his face relaxed as he replied, "Don't you think it's time we did?"

"Yes, I do," I admitted.

Mike drew closer, carefully, trying not to capsize the canoe. I stretched to meet him, face tilting...

And we flinched as our hats collided.

"Damn Red Sox," Mike said, sliding off both our hats and dropping them in the hull.

Before I could object to him dissing my team, Mike's lips pressed against mine, the force knocking me off balance. One of his arms caught me and slowed my descent, but not slow enough for my protesting knees. Feet stuck beneath me, I frantically straightened my legs to ease the pressure, kicking Mike hard enough for him to grunt into my mouth. My back pressed painfully against the seat behind me, the wooden edge digging into the space between my vertebrae.

Without Mike's expert handling, the canoe was no longer tracking in the gentle current, but we ignored the stern drifting sideways. It was harder to ignore the canoe's lurch as Mike stretched out a leg and fell to his elbows on my chest. Not in a good way. Now it was my turn to grunt.

"Sorry," Mike murmured.

"Shut up," I said, pulling his face back to me until his forehead rested against mine. His lips had been so warm, I couldn't imagine why I was shivering.

"Do you know how long I've wanted to—"

"Yes," I said. Because I did know. I remembered the first moment I'd seen him, wreathed in office pallor, and all of the times since then—in hospitals and diners and bars and even in his apartment—that he'd been there for me in every way except one. I reached up to grab his hair and missed; it was shorter than he usually wore it.

He pulled away. "Maybe we should —"

"Unless we're about to go over a waterfall," I said, pausing to get my breath, "and I hear those are in pretty short supply in Florida, we're doing exactly what we need to be."

I wished I could see his eyes behind his sunglasses. Mike got to his knees and reached for his paddle as the canoe went fully broadside across the river. "Hold that thought."

He executed a few strokes of some sort (I couldn't say which letter, but I knew the one that ran through my mind) and got the nose heading in the right direction. Briefly. Instead of continuing downstream, he paddled toward the shore on the right where another smaller, sandy-bottomed launch lay ahead.

The current had picked up. Mike's paddle dug deep and he let out a soft groan of effort as he said, "You won't threaten my masculinity if you decide to help."

I could take a hint. I jammed myself in the ribs pulling my paddle free, but I got a few good strokes in on the opposite side before feeling the soft bump of the sandy bottom beneath us. I soaked my socks and sneakers when I hopped out, scrambling ashore with the bow loop in one hand. Mike followed on my heels, and together we dragged the canoe above the waterline.

Flopping on the sand where it was relatively dry, I shivered and said, "Holy shit, my feet are freezing!"

"I'll bet I can warm them up," Mike said.

"Really?"

Mike blushed. "That's not what I meant." He pointed toward his bag in the canoe. "I have a thermos of hot coffee, although you might not want to drink out of your river cup now. Look, I didn't just bring you out here so I could jump your bones in the wilderness. Not that I don't want to—"

"Except maybe for the wilderness part," I interrupted, scratching where something had chewed on a section of exposed calf.

"Except maybe for the wilderness part," he agreed. "I

know this has been a long time coming, that it seems like we've been dancing around each other forever. I regret that. But I don't want to go from one extreme to the other."

"Because this is our first date," I said.

He grinned and lounged, hands supporting him on the sand. "Yeah, it is. How about that?"

I scooted across the ground toward him, grateful that my tights were snug enough to keep the grit out, until we were hip to hip. A slight breeze picked up, and I fought to secure my loose, wily curls behind my ears. "So what do you think is appropriate for a first date?"

Mike traced the entire perimeter of my ear, from where it attached at the skull all the way around to the hanging lobe, before contributing a curl to the hair-tucking. I resisted a strong urge to trace the bridge of his narrow nose in turn (after removing his damned sunglasses), from the spot that often crinkled between his brows to the tip where it flattened almost into a tiny cleft.

"Well, I did bring food," he said, interrupting my reverie.

"The way to this woman's heart," I acknowledged.

"And I may have even brought adult beverages. I trust you can control yourself, because I hear riverside picnics can get downright bacchanalian. But if you can't..."

He shrugged, and his face inched closer, until I could smell the citrus of his shaving cream and a not unpleasant hint of coffee from his breath.

"Hey!" A strange voice rang out. "You, with the canoe!"

I looked out over the water first, hopeful the unidentified man was talking to a passerby. No such luck—the river was deserted. "Are you rolling your eyes behind those badass sunglasses?" I asked.

Mike winced. "Only if you are."

Together, we turned toward the slight rise of the river-bank to see a big man in his early twenties, wearing a T-shirt and flannel shirt over jeans, swaggering toward us. Everything about him suggested rectangles—his boxy body shape, huge blocky sunglasses that looked stolen from an optometrist's office, and a tall, squared-off trucker's cap that held down his nearly shoulder-length, dirty brown hair. A few bits of brown, dead vegetation lay scattered across his shirt. Something about him was off. I couldn't put my finger on it, but when you're a petite woman who doesn't (usually) carry a firearm, you learn to listen to your instincts.

"Hey! You're not gonna believe this—"

For the record, beginning with that statement is not the best way to foster credibility.

"—But somebody just stole my car."

"I don't trust this guy," I murmured to Mike.

"You just don't want to share your picnic with him," he said, just as softly.

"And you do?"

"Good point," Mike acknowledged. He stood slowly, before offering me an arm up. His hands made an abrasive, swishing sound as he casually brushed the sand off his pants. Smiling apologetically as the man approached, Mike said, "Sorry, but we don't even have cell phones. I'm afraid there's not much we can do for you."

The younger man shook his head. "Yeah, the asshole stole my cell phone, too." He looked at me. "Sorry, ma'am."

And now I was a ma'am. Also not the best way to get a thirty-something woman on your side.

"Well, I hate to mess up your plans, but I was wondering if I could catch a ride with y'all. In your canoe," he continued, as if to avoid confusion with the Porsche we'd parked next to our water-going vessel. "I'm Emmett, by the way."

"Where?" Mike asked.

"Downstream." We were too stupefied to answer, so he added, "I figure there's got to be somebody at one of them launches, somebody who could give me a ride to a police station or at least call it in or something."

I waited, silent. This was Mike's date, his decision.

"Okay," Mike said.

Except I didn't think he'd make that one.

"But we're not taking you downstream. We just passed a big launch that's close to the highway, not a quarter mile back. We'll paddle back upstream, and if there's nobody there, it shouldn't take you long to find help once you start walking."

The man dropped his head, and I could see the muscles in his jaw working. I expected him to object, but a moment later, he said, "Fair enough. Let's go."

So much for listening to my instincts.

4

"You're not gonna believe this, but I ain't never been canoeing before," the man said from the bow.

This time I did believe him, despite the linguistic red flag. My knees and chest were spattered with cold water from his awkward strokes. Mike had suggested Emmett take my paddling spot to better balance the canoe, and our new friend had agreed.

With nothing better to do, I reflected on the arrangement. Although a few inches shorter than Mike, Emmett was much thicker, and I'd guess he weighed at least twenty-five pounds more. I wasn't exactly an expert, but it seemed to me the canoe would be most stable with Emmett's weight in the center. He could have been chivalrous, but I suspected Mike's real motivation for the arrangement was to keep Emmett busy and prevent him from sitting between us. I certainly didn't want the man at my back.

The graceless man should have seemed bumbling, and he was on the surface. But everything he said or did seemed to go no deeper than the surface. So what was below that? I wasn't sure I wanted to find out.

"Don't suppose y'all got any beer tucked away in here?" Emmett asked.

"No," Mike and I said in unison.

"Too bad. I know it's early, but a man could work up a thirst like this. It ain't as easy as it looks," he panted, glancing over his shoulder at me.

I nodded, but kept my mouth shut. He adjusted his jeans on his thighs and billowed the front of his T-shirt back and forth a few times. As warm as he was, he should have removed the flannel shirt. But he didn't, and I didn't like that.

The rusty old bridge lost some of its charm with me sitting upright, behind an uninvited guest on an unplanned return trip. The alligator I'd admired on our way downriver was still basking on the same log, squinting at us but not concerned enough to blink. Emmett stopped paddling long enough to raise a pistol finger at the reptile. I found myself wishing the big, scaly guy was in the mood for a snack.

Suddenly the canoe veered across the river toward the beast, and I wondered if Mike was thinking the same thing.

"Are you trying to get us killed?" Emmett demanded.

The canoe rocked gently as Emmett and I twisted to look at Mike in the stern. Emmett's eyes went wide with the motion, and I was afraid he'd drop his paddle in the river. But Mike calmly continued his measured, rhythmic strokes.

"Believe it or not," Mike began (his choice of words was no doubt for my benefit), "if you hug the bank, sometimes you can catch the current heading back up in the opposite direction. I'm just trying to save us a little work."

Emmett didn't look happy about it, but he shut his mouth and went back to paddling, albeit on the side farthest from the gator.

"Besides," Mike added, "no bigger than he is, he won't take more than a finger or two."

I might not trust Emmett, but I shouldn't let him get under my skin. I grinned and reached back to squeeze Mike's bony shin. Soon it would just be the two of us again, and I felt pretty good about that. Noel was right about my ill-advised romantic choices—Glenn, JD, and on and on all the way back to my teenaged years. (It was one of Lisa's favorite Listen to Your Big Sister lectures.) Mike was a good, kind man, and he was attractive to boot. Dating long distance would be a bit of a pain, but I was willing to give it a shot if he was, and it seemed as though he finally was.

My hat felt gross, damp from lying in the bottom of the canoe. I peeled it from my head and was blinded by the sun glaring off the water, even through my sunglasses. I squeezed and shook out my cap before battling the breeze for a slightly different hair configuration. Once I accomplished that, there was nothing more for me to do. I closed my eyes and luxuriated in the sun warming my face while its UV rays besieged my sunscreen. The crisp rustling of palmettos on the shore was so peaceful. That is, when it wasn't drowned out by Emmett's panting. Damned mouth-breather.

The canoe swung across the river again, this time because the launch was in sight. My spirits lifted, along with my butt. I'd been sitting on my feet, and the trip upstream had taken just long enough (fifteen minutes?) for my legs to fall asleep and grow damp from the life jacket beneath them.

In front of me, Emmett's shoulders tensed as I shimmied my lower half, stimulating the circulation. Maybe he couldn't swim. Except if he couldn't, you'd think he would've asked for a life jacket. Maybe he was just afraid of the water critters.

The haul-out was another sloping, sandy bottom. I braced myself as the canoe bumped and slid a couple of feet higher before coming to an abrasive stop. Emmett stepped clumsily onto the wet sand, trying to clear the edge of the water, and inadvertently kicked the canoe away. Still holding a paddle in one hand, he grabbed the bow line with the other and dragged the canoe higher, until the river lapped at the hull next to the forward seat. I waited for Emmett to thank us—or at least thank Mike—and to hand me the paddle. Instead, he walked away.

"I was hoping you could come with me. You know, in case somebody is here," Emmett called over his shoulder, still carrying the paddle. I followed.

"Syd, wait!" Mike yelled from behind.

Oh sure, he'd been perfectly fine with inviting strangers into our canoe, but now he wanted to show some common sense. I stalked after Emmett, annoyed at both men. "Hey! I need that paddle."

Emmett crossed the parking lot toward a black SUV with roof racks, the paddle slung over his shoulder and me on his heels. "Hey!" I yelled. "Just because you're having a shitty day doesn't mean we have to have one, too."

Emmett continued to ignore me, and I paid it forward by continuing to ignore Mike as he yelled for me. Emmett finally stopped in front of the abandoned SUV. One door was open, and debris—some the usual car crap, some of it more unusual—spilled out. Emmett picked up a long, black nylon strap with a sliding metal buckle from the ground. I wanted a closer look inside, but as I hunched forward I felt Mike's hand on my arm.

"Syd, I don't think we need to be messing with this," he said.

He was right; it looked like a crime scene. A minor crime scene (no blood and guts), but a crime scene nonetheless. The storage pouches on the backs of the seats had been sliced, as had portions of the upholstery. Fabric and stuffing made up much of the debris that spilled from the SUV. Even the folding windshield sunscreens hadn't escaped the blade. And in Florida, destroying a person's sunscreen is cold.

"It looks like they got this one, too," Emmett said from behind me.

I shuffled sideways to create some space between us, but I could see him while I watched Mike circle the vehicle. A sticker on the back glass with a familiar logo caught my eye, but before I could take a better look, Mike had made his way back around to us.

"You're probably right," he said. "But they definitely didn't stick around, so you should be fine. Good luck getting your car back. Now if you'll give us that paddle, we'll be on our way."

Mike extended a hand, and Emmett stared at it, as though it were covered in something nasty.

"Seriously? You're going to just leave me here?" Emmett asked, shaking his head. "I can't believe you people."

But he wasn't really surprised, any more than he'd really been surprised to find the torn-up vehicle. Mike took a step closer to him, arm still outstretched. My self-defense instructor Vince's instructions tumbled through my mind, and as always, I wished I'd paid more attention and gone to more classes. Still, I'd gone to enough to know to watch the man's hips. The first move Emmett made toward Mike, I'd take out the knee closest to me with a hard kick. In theory.

"All right. Fine. Be that way," Emmett said, and tossed the paddle to Mike.

I half-expected him to attack, but he didn't.

Mike caught the paddle in one hand, but his eyes never left Emmett. Apparently, he didn't trust the man any more than I did, and he was as reluctant as I was to assume Emmett would now go on his merry way. I heard a car in the distance and listened to it fade away. Nothing else. Just us. Maybe I was paranoid.

I gave Emmett a wide berth as I slowly moved around him to Mike's side. Mike's paddle-less arm encouraged me toward the river, but without actually touching me. Again, I wasn't the only one who was paranoid.

We were just about to turn our back on Emmett when a cell phone rang. Emmett's cell phone, the one that had supposedly been stolen. He pulled it from a pocket.

"Yeah," he said, voice hard and far less bumbling than it had been with us.

"Keep walking casually back to the canoe," Mike said softly. "Don't run."

And we did. But something about Mike's tone made me think he wasn't just being cautious; he knew something. "What'd you see in that SUV?"

"Not what—who," he said, and his hand briefly touched the small of my back before he remembered to keep it free. "It belongs to Levi."

"Who's—" But then I remembered, Levi was Sharkey's first name. And no one seemed to know where Sharkey had gone. I caught my toe on the ground, trying to suppress my instinct to run.

"Shit." Emmett's voice carried to us easily. "Okay."

Had his voice moved? Was he following us?

"I said okay." His voice was louder now, but not necessarily because he was closer; he sounded angrier, too. "Fine... *Fine!* I'll see you there."

Emmett sighed and let out one final, "Shit."

He was definitely following us. I looked toward Mike, and Emmett yelled, "Hey!"

Mike shook his head, but I couldn't help turning to see the man bearing down upon us. That's when Emmett pulled a handgun from behind his back and pointed it at me.

I stopped and raised hands that had suddenly gone numb. "Goddamned flannel shirt," I muttered.

5

"I was hoping we could do this the easy way," Emmett said, advancing on us. "You know, I get where I want to go and you guys do the right thing and feel like Good Samaritans, have a story to tell your friends. But no, you had to be assholes. Why did you have to be assholes?"

"Perhaps the better question is, why did you have to pick such assholes?" Mike asked. He'd stopped when I did, but took a half-step away from me now.

I knew what he was doing. Of course, so did Emmett. Or whatever the hell his name was. "Hunh-unh," he said. "You can cozy right back up next to your girlfriend there. And head back to the goddamned canoe."

"I can paddle us just as fast if you leave her behind. Probably faster," Mike said.

"What happened to 'it won't take you long to find help this close to the road'? You think I'm gonna leave her behind so she can do that?"

"Her legs are shorter than yours," Mike countered. "She's a slow walker."

If I'd been less terrified, I would have been more pissed.

"I said move, goddammit!" Emmett swung the gun toward the vessel, as if we'd forgotten where we left it. He'd probably gotten all of his gun handling skills from watching TV; I'd keep that in mind.

Mike and I looked at each other. A brow raised above the top of his sunglasses and he shrugged, as if to say, *What the hell else are we going to do?* I could think of plenty of things, but the first step in all of them was *freak out*, so I tried not to think at all. Just for a couple of minutes, until my heart could resume a normal rhythm and the desert in my mouth could blow away. I also tried to not look at the gun, and to breathe while not looking at said gun. I must not have been doing very well at either because I felt lightheaded.

"Syd!" Mike said, drawing my attention back to him. "You okay?"

I swallowed, as best I could with my damn sticky throat, and nodded. *Focus on where you are now*, I told myself, *not where you've been*. Besides, I'd gotten myself out of those crazy situations, or I wouldn't be around to get into this one. Hardly seemed fair though. This time, I hadn't even done anything stupid.

"Why don't you just take the SUV?" Mike asked. "It'd be a helluva lot faster than a canoe."

It was a good question. And the fact that I could recognize it was a good question meant I'd passed the palpitations and was ready to think again. For now.

"You got a key?" the man calling himself Emmett asked. "Because I sure as hell don't know how to hot-wire it. What do you think I am, a car thief?"

Mike stared at the gun. At least I assumed that's what he was staring at, since his face was pointing that direction and I knew I couldn't take my eyes off it. He asked, "What if I can hot-wire it?"

"Just get in the damned canoe."

It wasn't far back to the launch, but Mike and I took our time, walking slowly side-by-side with Emmett following. The whole way, I prayed for someone to pull into the otherwise abandoned lot—preferably someone in law enforcement —but no such luck.

When we reached the canoe, Mike dropped the cursed paddle into the bow. We'd be halfway home by now (or better yet, getting chewed up by creepy crawlies while we made out in the bushes) if I'd just let Emmett leave with the damn thing and made Mike muscle us out alone.

Mike's pants swished as he stepped in, bracing himself on the gunwales against the wobble as he crept toward the stern, then sat facing us in the back seat. I started to follow, but Emmett grabbed my arm.

"Wait," he said. "This is how we're gonna do it. Red—"

"My name is Sydney, not Red." It hadn't always been easy growing up with flaming hair. As an adult, there were very few people I allowed to call me that, and that select group did not include individuals who pointed guns at me.

Emmett shoved me by the arm. I staggered, but kept my balance.

"Stand right there," he said. "I'll get in next. If you take a step toward me, I'm shooting your boyfriend in the guts. Then we'll see who's fucking red."

I surveyed the parking area one last, lonely time. Still no cavalry. The scrub to the left was thick, but a worn trail led downriver, presumably to the next launch rather than the nearest police station. There was nothing I could do except pray the asshole slipped while getting in and shot himself. Unfortunately, that didn't happen. The nylon strap he'd retrieved from the SUV dangled below his shirt in the back. He fished it from a pocket one-handed and tossed it to Mike. "Wrap this around your feet in a figure-eight. And you better pull it snug, or I will."

Mike did as he'd instructed, twisting awkwardly around sneakers the size of small boats. Emmett then ordered him to stretch out his legs and, kneeling in the center, checked the spacing between his feet. Mike winced when Emmett yanked the binding tighter. A couple feet of extra strap hung from the end.

"Now tie this to that wooden piece there," Emmett said, pointing at the yoke with the strap. Mike did some kind of elaborate knotting, and once again, Emmett gave it a tug to make sure it was secure.

The extra precaution made me uneasy. Mike and I are both strong swimmers and comfortable in the water, so if we capsized, he could probably get free before drowning. Assuming we had nothing else on our minds at the time, like potentially being shot. But the sight of my date with bound feet tied to the canoe made it impossible not to worry about Emmett's endgame—were we simply postponing the inevitable by playing along? Especially since, if this guy really did have some connection with Mike's friend Sharkey, it's likely we had the same final destination.

"Good," Emmett said, still facing Mike. "We're gonna make our way downriver until I say stop. That means I'll be sitting with my back to you and my gun pointing at her. I'm gonna tell you now, if you try anything, I got no qualms about putting a bullet in the back of her pretty little head. You got that?"

Mike's jaw clenched. "I got it."

Emmett shifted to keep an eye on Mike while pointing the gun at me. "All aboard," he said.

I stretched a leg over the side, and the canoe began sliding off the bank as soon as I put my weight on it, forcing me to do a split. "Dammit," I muttered, hopping one-legged on the sand, trying not to fall on the jerk's gun as I flopped the rest of the way into the canoe.

"Graceful much?" he asked.

I held my tongue. I must be maturing, or maybe I just wasn't ready to die.

Mike back-paddled, maneuvering us into the center of the river. My own paddle sat in the hull, and I pulled it toward me carefully to clear the seats and yoke, pausing as it came free. If only it were wooden, something with some heft... but I couldn't do any damage with what was essentially a hollow, plastic stick. Emmett watched me—or perhaps the renegade thoughts crossing my face—and waited. Finally, I faced front and began paddling.

The sensation of a gun pointing at the space between my shoulder blades made me short of breath. Sweat broke out in the armpits of my long-sleeved T-shirt. Panic was not helpful. I concentrated on the feel of the blade dragging through the water, on the constant, reassuring resistance of the fluid, on the light that flashed from the river in little pockets and the flight of a hawk as it cruised above us until it disappeared from view. Eventually, the anxiety receded. Still, I knew I'd smell ripe by the end of the day. I just hoped I was in a condition then to care.

I was relieved to see our alligator friend had vacated his basking spot. The couple of turtles that had taken up residence there seemed less likely to draw Emmett's ire, and his gunfire. I didn't know how many bullets his gun held, but undoubtedly there'd still be enough left for Mike and me after he took potshots at the local wildlife.

As the sun rose higher in the sky, I found myself sweating for reasons that had nothing to do with anxiety. It felt good, doing something physical. I mean, it would if I didn't have a gun at my back. The canoe rocked when Emmett shifted behind me.

"At least I can take this damn hot shirt off now," he said.

I glanced over my shoulder at him, at his pale, beefy arms

sticking out from his short sleeves. I hoped he got sunburned and wished he was wearing a tank top. But he was quiet, and that was a relief. Although if he kept talking, maybe I'd get some clue to who he was and what he wanted.

What did I know so far? Forget *knowing*... I'd settle for best guesses. Emmett hadn't started out at the launch where we'd picked him up. From the state of his clothes, I'd say he tramped through the woods to that launch from the parking lot with the SUV. From the state of the SUV, I'd say he didn't leave it until he'd given up on finding whatever he was looking for inside. So what was he looking for? And where was the vehicle's owner, Levi Sharkey?

It seemed likely Mike's friend had a good excuse for not meeting us this morning. If he'd been driving his own vehicle when it was trashed, I had two reasons for believing Sharkey had gotten away. First, I hadn't noticed any blood in the SUV, and if Mike had, he hadn't bothered to mention it. Second, Emmett was still pursuing something—and downriver—so it seemed likely Sharkey had escaped via canoe. (The vehicle had roof racks and straps, so it could have easily carried a canoe or kayak.) But was Emmett pursuing Sharkey because the man had something he wanted, or simply because he was an almost-victim/witness? In other words, was Sharkey specifically targeted, or was he in the wrong place at the wrong time? I leaned toward the former—it seemed like an odd place to be by happenstance. It made me wonder how well Mike knew the man, and what his old friend had gotten himself into. And if Sharkey had escaped downriver, what would Emmett do if we found him?

I paused to adjust my cap and wipe the sweat from my forehead. While I was at it, I took a swig from a water bottle stashed in the bow. The cool liquid sluicing down my parched throat felt pretty damned amazing.

"More paddling, less wool-gathering up there," Emmett said.

I took another sip of water and flipped him the finger before complying. If he saw it, he didn't say anything. Or maybe, like me, he was picking his battles.

My hair hung through the back of my hat in a loose ponytail, and I could feel the sweat gathering at the base of my skull. As it crawled down my neck, I wondered how much of my sunscreen was going with it. I doubted Emmett would be willing to stop while I reapplied. Too bad, because what we needed to do was slow this crazy train (canoe) down. Nothing good could come of us apprehending Sharkey. So what would Emmett be willing to stop for?

"I have to pee," I said.

"Nobody's stopping you," Emmett replied.

"You really want me to pee in the canoe you're sitting in?"

He snorted. "It'd take a lot of goddamn pee to make it all the way back here to my feet, and I don't see how you got that much in you. So if you want to pee your pants and sit in it for however long, you go right ahead."

So much for that idea. And short of convincing an alligator to jump in our canoe, I had nothing else.

I don't know how long we'd been paddling—I rarely wore a watch—but soon my arms were feeling it, burning and sluggish. I was out of shape. We entered an area with even denser vegetation than what we'd passed so far. Heavy limbs arced overhead, providing a bit of welcome shade, and some sort of evergreen shrubbery encroached from the banks. A gap appeared ahead of us to the right, and Emmett said, "Head in there."

I eased up on my own strokes, afraid of overpowering Mike's steering. I needn't have worried—he probably could have handled the tandem canoe singlehanded. The opening was at least a couple of car lengths, and he swung us easily through the gap in the greenery. A short channel, maybe twenty-five yards, led to a broad, clear-watered spring. I could distinguish lumps in the sand beneath us, and as the water grew deeper near the center, it became a beautiful aquamarine blue, as if a tiny Caribbean Sea had been plopped in the middle of an inland river.

"Wow," I whispered.

"Yeah," came Mike's hushed, reverent answer.

We'd both stopped paddling and gazed over the side into the depths. I trailed a finger in the cold water as the current carried us toward another wall of vegetation at the back of the spring. There was rustling on the bank, but I didn't see anything. Maybe there were armadillos in the forest.

"All right, that's enough sightseeing," Emmett said. "Let's back on out of here."

I rested my paddle across the gunwales as Mike maneuvered us from the stern. Exiting took more effort than entering had. Instead of turning smoothly, the canoe drifted to a stop before it began reversing. I was curious how Mike managed it and knew I should be studying his movements and taking mental notes, but I couldn't. My eyes were glued to the jungle around us, little hairs standing up on my neck. I couldn't shake the feeling that we were being watched from the shore.

6

"**G**oddamn, I'm hungry. What do you have to eat in there?" Emmett asked, reaching for the bag behind him.

"Not much that you can eat in a moving canoe, or without utensils," Mike said. His voice had an edge, but the rhythmic sound of his strokes didn't change.

"Well, we're not stopping," Emmett said. "And obviously I need something I can eat one-handed."

"You'll find some granola bars in the smaller bag."

Soon I heard a wrapper crinkling. I quickly shifted my hands and gripped midway down the shaft of my paddle to jab Emmett with the solid, knobby end. Glancing over my shoulder—

"Safety's off, finger's on the trigger," Emmett said, staring at me with the gun steady and an open granola bar on his lap. "You want to try it, you go right ahead."

Instead I adjusted my hands and continued paddling. If Mike and I were getting out of this, it'd have to be onshore. Making a move while we were in the canoe was too risky for both of us. Since Emmett wouldn't stop to pee or to eat, it seemed the only time we'd be onshore was the moment we found Sharkey. Or whatever else he was looking for. We'd have to be ready.

I hadn't yet shaken the sense of being watched, though I hadn't seen any evidence of it. It didn't make sense, either. Emmett was obviously working with someone—or maybe more accurately, *for* someone. I'd gotten the impression from the brief call earlier that Emmett was not the one making the decisions, but rather the one following orders. But his associate wouldn't be watching us from the shore, especially if his wilderness skills were anything like Emmett's appeared to be.

That left Sharkey, but he had no reason to linger. Unless he wasn't the person Mike thought he was, but instead was a rival of some kind, targeting Emmett. Or it was someone else entirely. No matter who it was, why keep shadowing us? Why not just take Emmett out? I guessed I'd just have to wait and see. But I've never had the type of disposition that deals well with unknowns.

"Mike, what did you make us for lunch?" I asked. Steak seemed unlikely, but it'd be nice to know if we had any pointy utensils.

"Oh no, you don't," he answered, his voice pitched to carry. "You'll just have to wait and see."

"No talking," Emmett said. "Not to each other."

Downstream, the river curved sharply. I hoped closer to the road, but I hadn't heard any cars for a while. Trees hugged the shoreline, making it difficult to see what lay ahead.

"Why'd you bring the food?" Emmett asked. Maybe he was feeling the need to bolster his focus as much as I was. And maybe, just maybe, that gun hand was getting tired.

"I brought food because this was my idea. You've interrupted our first date."

"No shit?" Emmett laughed. "What do you think the chances are of getting a second one?"

"That remains to be seen," Mike said.

"Like so many things," Emmett answered. He wiggled a little behind me, rocking the canoe, and continued talking to Mike, which was the best of both worlds. It gave me some sense of what was going on behind me, and meant the man with the gun was ignoring me, or at least discounting me as a threat. "What made you want to go canoeing, instead of just a movie or something?"

Mike took so long to answer I didn't think he would. Finally, he said, "I think Syd and I are a little past the dinner and a movie stage."

I couldn't help but smile.

We floated steadily toward the river bend, curving so subtly I wasn't sure if our progress was the result of Mike's gentle navigation or simply the current carrying us along. Inch by inch, the slow reveal of what lay ahead was... more trees. More tan water. A resumption of a straightened river course. No road. No launches. No police boat. If there was such a thing in this part of the state.

"You're not local, but you're not tourists, either," Emmett said. "How'd you get here?"

"Drove from Tallahassee," Mike said. "A friend knew somebody from one of the outfitters out of Marianna who was willing to help us out. They're supposed to pick us up downstream."

"Where at?"

"I don't know. I don't remember the name of the spot, and it's not like there's gonna be a sign. They said we'd see them. Or they'll see us."

"All day trip?"

"Half day."

"You might just be a hair late," Emmett said. "What do you do during the week?"

"We both work for the Leg," Mike said.

That being the *Ledge*, not a limb or something precarious to stand upon but short for legislature, and—like most of what Mike had said so far—a total lie. I'd never heard Mike in prevaricating mode before. The man had skills. In addition to the ones that kept the canoe moving smoothly past another submerged log. I blinked against an unexpected glare off the water as we swung around the obstruction.

"Which side?" Emmett asked. Meaning, which party, Republican or Democrat.

"There are sides?" Mike asked, deadpan.

"Fair point," Emmett snorted. "You ever been married?"

It was such a non sequitur, the only thing that shocked me more than the question was Mike's reply.

"Once," he said, voice gruff.

I swung to face him, leaning sideways to see around Emmett's fat head. "You've been married before?"

Mike didn't immediately respond, and paranoia of a different sort kicked in. "You're not still married, are you?"

"No!" he said. "Not for a while."

"How long is a while?" I asked, gripping my paddle so tightly I could feel scratches on the surface of the shaft.

"Not long enough," Mike said, with a sense of finality.

Was he lying? Was this mysterious former marriage part of the elaborate story-spinning for Emmett's benefit? If so, Mike was the best liar I'd ever met. Which, being in my business, was saying something.

"Okay, as amusing as this is, you need to turn your ass around and paddle," Emmett said to me, motioning with his gun, his elbow resting upon his knee. "The sooner we do, the sooner you can get somewhere suitable for a proper interrogation."

I could hear the laughter in his voice. *Asshole.*

"Not long enough, like it was last week or last year or last century?" I resumed.

"I said—" Emmett began.

"I'm paddling!" I yelled, forgetting I shouldn't antagonize the man with the gun.

Mike's response was almost inaudible over the roaring in my ears. "It became official last year."

Last year. *Jesus.* Before or after we'd met? It had to be before. I thought back to his demeanor then—even to his physical appearance—and pieces started to come together. References he'd made to Richard helping him out recently, to the amount of time he'd spent with him and his wife and the quality of her cooking. His unusual pallor, saying he'd gone through a dry spell lately on outdoor excursions. The apartment that was perfectly fine but not particularly personalized, and when he didn't seem like an apartment guy. More recently, the energy in Mike's voice when I'd asked about the health of Richard's marriage, and he'd replied who knew? That marriages were like black boxes. So what had happened in Mike's black box?

"Who did the leaving, you or the wife?" Emmett asked.

This time, Mike didn't answer.

"No comment? Well, I think we all know what that means, when a man would rather not say," Emmett observed. "And I think your chances of a second date just dropped like a stone."

Without thinking, I lifted my right hand from the paddle and flipped him the bird again. Emmett grabbed my forearm, yanked it toward him, and squeezed it hard enough to bring tears to my eyes. Trees blurred in my vision (*was that movement on shore? a flash of yellow?*) as I swung my head toward Emmett and twisted my shoulder, trying to ease the pressure.

"Do it again, and I will not hesitate to break that finger

for you, which'll make paddling a bitch." Emmett stared at me. I watched sweat trickle from his temple and gather in the stubble over his lip as he added, "And you in the back, Mr. Divorcé—you think I can't feel it when you stop paddling, think I can't see you in the reflection from her fancy sunglasses? Think again. Or a broken finger will be the least of your new girl's worries."

Mike resumed paddling, and the man released my arm, leaving white fingermarks that would be blue by nightfall. If we lived that long.

7

Emmett was right. There'd be time enough for interrogating Mike later, and my aching arm did a good job of helping me focus on the more important task at hand—staying alive. Had I really seen something in the woods when Emmett grabbed me? The yellow had been awfully bright for something found in nature, or for something inanimate that had been cast off and left to fade and rot outdoors. And I was certain there had been movement. But could the movement have been because *we* were moving and the object was fixed? It had also been low to the ground for a person. Perhaps it was a very careful person, or a brightly spray-painted armadillo. At this point, both options seemed equally likely.

My arm wasn't just aching from rough handling and physical exertion. I was hungry, and as usual, that hunger trickled down to the rest of my body in the form of exhaustion and muddled thinking. "Did you eat all those granola bars?" I asked, eyes still forward.

"They were a little on the grass and twigs side for me," Emmett said. "I suppose you think it's time to eat."

"She always thinks it's time to eat," Mike said.

"You know, I'm not sure you're helping your case, Mr. First Date," Emmett said.

For once, Emmett and I agreed, but I wasn't about to tell him that. "I don't know what the clock says, but add an hour for us because we're on Eastern time. And I didn't eat break-fast this morning with the expectation of a forced River March."

"All right," Emmett said, and I felt him shift slightly behind me. "Don't get stupid. And don't be taking forever."

I rested my paddle across the gunwales and rose to my knees.

"What'd I just say about being stupid?" he demanded.

"My legs went to sleep." It was true, and now that I could feel the blood returning to the large muscles, I was starting to wish they'd stayed that way. Pins and needles... I leaned forward and wiggled, shaking my head against the painful irri-tation. Something hit me in the ass, and I flinched, nearly knocking my paddle into the river.

"Don't sit on your lunch."

I retrieved the bar from beneath me, then shimmied a little before settling on the flat, wooden seat. Maybe I'd be more comfortable with the life jacket on top. Except then my butt would be wet.

"Your designated lunch break's about over, so you best be hurrying it up."

My fingers, cramped into position, seemed incapable of any task that was not holding a paddle. I nearly dropped the granola bar in the hull trying to peel it from the plastic, which may not have been a bad idea. The bar was dense and dry, with each bite requiring an accompanying sip of water. For the first time, I wondered how much water Mike had packed. Emmett had already claimed one bottle, while paddling upstream before he pulled the gun on us. I hoped we had a spare, especially if the rest of our provisions were anything like this chocolate flavored sawdust nugget. I wriggled my tongue around, trying to dislodge a persistent chunk of protein from my teeth. And that's when I noticed another flash up ahead—but not on the shore. On the river.

I wiped the corner of my mouth with the back of my wrist (*gross*), then rolled up the empty wrapper, trying not to let on that I'd seen anything. Turning, I found myself facing Emmett's gun again. One advantage of hunger was that it had helped me forget the gun at my back. Now I remembered. I raised my hands and held the wrapper between two slightly shaking fingers.

"Trash," I said.

"Do I look like the goddamned garbage man?" Emmett asked.

But he took the wrapper anyway, and his attention left me for a moment while he tucked it back in a bag. Hands still raised, I hooked a thumb toward the bow, and Mike gave a slight nod. Whatever it was, he'd seen it, too. This might be our opportunity.

"Does that mean it's my turn to eat?" Mike asked.

"Not until your girlfriend gets us going."

I began paddling mostly on the right side, hoping to block Emmett's sight line of the glint ahead without throwing us too far off course. And it was a glint, a bit of shiny metal reflection. I turned my head so I could see the men behind me in my peripheral vision, triggering an angry twinge in my neck as I plunged the paddle into the river on the next stroke.

Emmett kept his eyes on Mike—even tied to the canoe, he considered him more of a threat than me—and was likely to do so as long as I kept paddling and didn't hit anything. But I didn't see how Mike could stretch out eating one protein bar long enough for us to reach our target.

"How about another one?" Mike asked.

Well, that was one way.

Emmett tossed another bar through the air. "Consider this lunch and dinner."

We were close enough now for me to see the metal glint was an aluminum canoe snuggled up next to the low, sandy embankment. What I couldn't see was whether it was occupied. There was no one sitting upright in it, or anywhere on the shore nearby, but that didn't mean there wasn't someone lying in the hull.

I looked back sharply as Mike began coughing in the stern.

"Keep those arms moving, girlfriend," Emmett said. "He'll be fine. Damn hippie food."

I was torn between paddling as quickly as I could and watching a still-coughing Mike over my shoulder. He'd managed a few swigs from his water bottle, but it sounded as if that hadn't gone down the right way either. There is nothing like a fake coughing fit to trigger a real, uncontrollable coughing fit.

As we got closer to the shore and the strange canoe, small obstructions—rocks and bits of logs—began appearing in front of us as well. Zipping around them at the last second was beyond my skills, so I generally ran them over and hoped for the best. It seemed a solid strategy, until one of these obstacles made an audible—and butt discernible—thump.

"What did I say about the safety on this—"

Emmett broke off, torn between being pissed at me and excited by what he now saw lay ahead. "When were you gonna see fit to mention our friend parked up there?"

"I don't see anyone," I said, which was technically true.

"Well, he can't be far. All right back there, Meryl Streep. You can stop the dying act and help your girlfriend get us ashore in one piece."

Mike's hacking ceased (sneaky, faking bugger) and our course steadied with his hand. I held my breath as we approached the canoe, half-expecting someone to jump out of it like a haunted house coffin.

"Pull up alongside it," Emmett said.

It was empty except for a single bag, I realized, as we began to hit bottom. Not surprisingly, a vessel holding the three of us (especially Emmett) sat lower in the water than an empty one. The other canoe still floated, retreating a few inches when we bumped it. Someone had looped the bow line over a piece of driftwood—the better part of a dead tree, actually—stuck in the bank.

"Hand me the bag," Emmett said. "Slowly."

I shoved my paddle out of the way and dropped to my knees, leaning over the side. The bottom of our canoe scraped sideways—just an inch or two—across something embedded in the riverbank. Probably another chunk of dead tree. I hesitated, afraid of face-planting on the gunwale of the other canoe if ours moved again. But we stayed put, so I stretched out full-length, grunting as I lifted the bag by a strap. It was a small, cheap, gray duffel, water resistant but by no means waterproof. A dark stain a couple of inches in diameter shone wetly on one end. I avoided touching it as I dropped the bag in the space between me and Emmett. It thunked softly as it landed.

"Unzip it," he said.

I did (the track was a little sticky on one side), and started to reach inside.

"Hey! I didn't say put your grubby paws in it."

I raised my hands in apology and backed over my seat and into the narrow remaining space of the bow, to give the man with the gun more room. He waited until I sat on my feet (the hard, toothy edges of my sneaker tread pressed through my thin leggings), then pulled the mouth of the bag wide. He glanced up at me warily, but I kept my face passive and my gaze on Mike behind him. I couldn't imagine our play going forward. Mike's feet were still tied and secured to the yoke. And Emmett wasn't as fatigued as I'd hoped he'd be by now. Probably because we were doing all the damn work.

"Shit," Emmett said, dumping the bag.

A half-empty water bottle, a plastic cup that had once held cottage cheese, and a couple more snack bars tumbled free before he turned the bag inside out. He ran his hands over the fabric from end to end. I didn't know what he'd been hoping for, but obviously it wasn't there.

Emmett swept a hand across his sweaty face, then wiped it on his jeans. Sighing, he pulled out his cell phone and looked at the screen. "Sonofabitch," he said, squeezing the phone in his hand until I thought he'd throw it. Instead, he shoved it back in his pants and shook his head, seeming to regroup.

"Okay," he said. "Here's what we're going to do. Our friend couldn't have gone far, so we're going to find him."

I didn't personally know "our friend"—whether it was Sharkey or not—so I wasn't sure how I felt about this plan. But my feelings were about to be clarified.

"And by *we*," Emmett continued, turning toward Mike, "I mean me and your girlfriend. You're going to stay put. When we come back, if you're not here, or if I don't see your feet still tied to this canoe, I'll put a bullet in her brain. It's that simple. Are we clear?"

Mike's voice was husky when he said, "Crystal."

"Good," Emmett said, turning his attention to me. "Now let's go. Ladies first."

8

I stepped from the canoe on shaking legs. Emmett told me to secure it to the same driftwood forest as the other vessel. Once I'd done so, he followed and waved me toward the overgrown jungle. But first I indulged in one last look at Mike. He'd scooted his rear to the hull in front of his seat and stretched his long legs over the yoke. All he needed to complete the picture was a beer in his hand... and unbound feet. He gave me a thumbs-up, and I smiled. Or at least, I tried. The result was closer to a paralyzed rictus that might attract carrion birds.

"Move," Emmett said. "We don't have all day."

Funny—that's exactly what I was supposed to have had. *All day*, with no stress. *Asshole*. I banked my anger and started toward the forest, my feet slipping on the unstable sand of the gentle slope. The sun was high overhead, and I hesitated at the edge of the dappled shade, my eyes and brain momentarily stunned by the changing light.

"You know, the same goes for you," he said.

It took me a moment to process and find his conversational thread. "Behave or you'll kneecap him," I said. "I got it."

"Hey!" he barked, and I stopped walking. "You think I'm kidding?"

I turned to him, removed my sunglasses, and hung them from the front of my shirt. "No," I said, making no effort to mask the tremor in my voice. "I know you're not."

Then I swung around, before I could say something stupid (i.e., something that suggested the tremor was more anger than fear), and concentrated on finding the path, which was easier to do without the sunglasses. I wasn't exactly Daniel Boone, but I ought to be able to see which trail our "friend" had either taken or blazed on his way away from the river. Of course, I wasn't certain if that was a good thing or a bad thing, as I approached a well-trod area.

"This guy's not going to shoot me, is he?" I asked, shielding my face from a branch. I imagined it arcing to smack Emmett as I released it.

"He's not armed," Emmett said.

He sounded pretty certain.

A few yards farther in, I noticed a divot at the edge of the path, like a man's knees might make hitting the ground. "Is he injured?" I asked.

"He might be."

Might be. Emmett was either being coy about his injuries or he honestly didn't know. But I was pretty sure I did. I squatted down for a better look at the depression. The ground was soft, but more substantial here than it had been closer to the river. In a nearby, smashed area of something akin to grass, I saw a small smear of blood. Raising my head, my eyes followed a line of disturbed vegetation that stretched for another ten or fifteen yards.

"It's your show," I said, standing and casually trying to extricate a small burr without leaving a hole in my pants.

My goal wasn't to preserve my wardrobe, but rather to encourage Emmett to walk ahead of me. I wasn't about to run until he had something—or someone—else to occupy his attention, but as soon as he did, all bets were off. We weren't far from the river. If I yelled for Mike to get a head start paddling, I could swim out and catch up. Unless Emmett was a much better marksman than I suspected, it would be difficult for him to hit two moving targets with a handgun, while himself moving. That's assuming he'd leave Sharkey behind to chase me. If I made a clean initial getaway (let's not pretty it up—if I didn't get shot in the back at point-blank range), the next area that worried me was the transition from the shore to the deeper channel of the river. With no idea what the bottom was like, I had to trust that I could—

"Hey!" I yelled, as Emmett grabbed my arm and shoved me forward.

"Did you hear me?" he demanded.

I hadn't, planning my grand escape, but his intent was pretty clear. Had I just missed another opportunity, with the close contact? If I made it through this, my next self-defense class with Vince and Glenn would be a debriefing. I could hear Glenn drawl, *Here's what you should have done, darling.* Too bad his voice didn't keep speaking in my head and finish that thought with some instructions. With no other choice, I kept following the trail.

The man must have gotten to his feet again. A few paces later, I found another blood smear on a broad, waxy leaf at about my waist height. I squatted again and examined the ground, finding a few dark, wet drops for my trouble. Things were not looking good for Sharkey. Not that I had any room to talk.

Head down, watching for signs of his passing, I walked right into a tree branch. It knocked my cap from my head, but I was glad I hadn't lost an eye. I took advantage of the moment, while replacing my hat, to get oriented. Turning slowly in a circle, I realized that's exactly what we were doing —turning in a circle, albeit a larger one. Having drawn us away from the river, Sharkey was now heading back toward his canoe. Was he lying in wait, or had he simply hoped to gain some ground in his escape? Perhaps he wasn't badly injured, and he'd intended to paddle away with both canoes (not realizing that Emmett had left company in his). In that case, what would happen when he returned to the canoes and found my date? Mike would never leave me behind, but I had no reason to trust his friend's integrity. Assuming it even was his friend. Maybe Sharkey had loaned his SUV to someone else. And maybe he was already dead in a ditch.

No matter what lay ahead, we (meaning Mike and I) were better off getting there sooner rather than later. So I picked up the pace. Emmett didn't complain. With a distinct height disadvantage and fighting my way through occasional brambles, it's not like I was going to leave him behind.

Finally, I saw something lying on the ground ahead. And so did Emmett.

"Wait, slow down," he said.

I did, and I stopped when I reached the body. Because that's what it was—a body. Living or otherwise, I couldn't tell. It was a dark-haired man, stocky and a little below average height, lying facedown.

"Check him," Emmett said.

I turned to the man with the gun. "Do I look like an EMT?" I asked, and experienced a moment of déjà vu. Maybe I should add first responder training to my must-attend classes, right after self-defense.

Emmett stepped closer, but not so close as to be within range of my mad (that is, nonexistent) disarming skills, and shrugged. "Has it occurred to you that I don't need you? I could shoot you right here. Yeah, then I'd have to kill your boyfriend too, but all that means is I'm out two bullets and I have to paddle the fucking canoe. Inconvenient maybe, but what's only inconvenient for me is a significantly shittier day for you. Your last shitty day."

The sweat-drenched back of my neck suddenly felt cold. I wished I knew if Emmett were more than just a redneck punk in over his head. If he were, I'd be pretty sure he was bluffing. It'd be more than inconvenient to paddle a canoe downriver while holding a gun on Sharkey; it'd be impossible. Assuming, that is, Sharkey was still alive, and that Emmett had a reason to keep him that way. But a redneck punk in over his head doesn't make those kinds of calculations before pulling a trigger.

I approached the body carefully, as if the leaf litter concealed a nest of winter-dozing snakes. The man's left arm was crushed beneath him, and as I knelt next to him, my knees fit in the gap between his outstretched right arm and torso. Blood stained his shirt on that side, below a familiar logo. He was definitely still alive. His back rose and fell with his breath, probably more quickly than was healthy. Carotid or radial pulse? I needed to check if it was crazy skippy-dippy. I reached for his wrist, took it gently in my hands, and—

The bloody man twisted his arm to grab mine, then rolled over, taking me with him. He wasn't huge by any means, but his compact body was solid muscle, and in a flash he'd easily pinned me beneath him. One arm rested across my chest just below my clavicle, supporting much of his weight, and I couldn't draw breath. His other hand was at my throat. I felt a point against the delicate flesh where my jaw met my neck —another reason to not breathe.

"Back off!" the man yelled, presumably at Emmett, and presumably with no idea that I was Emmett's hostage as well. I prayed Emmett didn't shoot us both.

I tried to speak, but couldn't fill my lungs to do so,

inhaling just enough for the barest squeak of air to scrape through my throat. My eyes grayed around the edges and my chest grew tight, tighter, then started a choking spasm that forced the point of the knife to pierce my skin. The man's weight on me eased slightly, and I reached down to grab his crotch, squeezing desperately at whatever I could get my hand on through his jeans. His elbow jabbed painfully into my pec above my breast as he pushed himself away. I flailed, sucking wind and still unable to focus, and heard him yelp with pain.

Now it was my turn to scramble, on my hands and knees on the ground, but I didn't make it far. Emmett stopped me. I nearly grabbed his leg and gave it a yank before I saw his hands and *gun* penetrated the adrenaline coursing through my veins.

"Don't move," Emmett said.

I gasped for breath, forearms on the ground, while Emmett stepped around me and gave the prone man a solid kick to the ribs, right in the bloody area. The injured man moaned and rolled on his side, folding. Somehow he'd managed to hold onto his weapon, an open pocketknife about two or three inches long, until Emmett stepped on his arm and retrieved the blade.

"Where is it?" Emmett demanded.

No response.

Emmett wiped the knife on his pants automatically before closing it one-handed against his leg and securing the weapon in his own back pocket. Then he told me to get up. I hesitated, frontal brain stalled out, and he repeated, "Get up."

My pulse pounded in my skull. I leaned against a pine tree, squeezing its textured bark beneath my hand as I stood, trying to ground myself in the physical here and now, and to control the shaking.

"You're bleeding," he added.

My hand strayed toward my throat, but pulled away before touching it. I doubted I was bleeding much, and the last thing the tenuous hold on my composure needed to look at was a hand covered in my blood. Instead, I looked at the man on the ground. Curled on his side in the leaf litter, his body had relaxed, possibly unconscious.

Emmett was already pointing the gun at me, but he lifted and lowered it for emphasis and said, "Stay."

I did, while he frisked the man on the ground. Sharkey groaned, but his body rolled easily for Emmett to gain access to the pockets beneath him. Still empty-handed, Emmett shook his head and muttered in frustration, but he didn't seem all that surprised.

"What now?" I asked, regretting the words as soon as they'd left my mouth. It still felt like a two-by-four smacked me in the chest with every other beat of my heart.

Emmett swiped his free arm across his sweaty face. "Now, you get him up."

I looked at the man on the ground. He'd progressed to moaning, but was nowhere near sitting up. And I doubted he was more than five foot eight, but I'd already felt how dense he was. He'd be damned heavy as almost-dead weight.

"Are you kidding me?" I asked.

Emmett tilted his head and his gun, like he'd no doubt seen people do on TV. Right before shooting someone. "Would you rather be left behind?"

9

Well, shit.

W I grabbed my hat from the ground, shoved my hair back inside, and clung to anger (my Red Sox cap was taking a lot of abuse today) to keep the fear at bay. Then I nudged the prone man with my toe. His eyes opened, and I waited a moment for him to get past fight-or-flight and reconsider the idea of attacking the closest person. Again.

"What's his name?" I called over my shoulder, as if I didn't have a pretty good idea.

"Puddin tane," Emmett said. "What the hell difference does it make?"

I bit my lip. *There's a gun at your back, don't be a smartass... don't give him an excuse.* Instead, I squatted next to the man on the ground, trying to penetrate the haze without entering striking range.

"Hey, dude," I began, only to stall out when my brain snagged on *who the hell says dude anymore?* Probably a sign that I needed to hydrate. "I'd appreciate it if you don't hit me—or stab me, for that matter—because I don't want to be here any more than you do."

The man still looked woozy, but his eyes focused on me briefly before skittering toward Emmett at my back. Then his gaze returned to my neck. "Sorry about that," he said.

"Whatever." I wasn't ready to let him off the hook for that one, but I'd wait until we weren't being held at gunpoint to raise it again. I settled my sunglasses back on my face, wary of them being crushed. "I'm supposed to help you up. What do you think the chances are of that happening?"

He sat up slowly, wincing as he did. His voice was surprisingly deep, with a crisp, non-Southern edge, when he responded, "I guess we both better hope they're good."

It wasn't pretty, and by the end I wore nearly as much of his blood as he did, but he was upright. I moved to his less bloody left side and wedged my shoulders beneath his outstretched arm. We remained hunched, but not painfully so because he only had about half a foot of height advantage over me.

No one spoke on the way back to the canoes—the injured man and I were working too hard, and really, what did Emmett need to say? We were closer to the river than I'd thought, but I could feel Emmett getting impatient on our heels. We'd strayed slightly off-trail, and the last section required more effort and more swatting plant crap out of the way. (Botanist, I am not.) With all of the branchy interference, I might've been able to make a run—and swim—for it, if a bloody guy weren't hanging on me. But it would've been a near thing, and if I'd had any doubts about Emmett's willingness to inflict harm, the condition of the man next to me had convinced me otherwise. Plus, having now met Sharkey—because really, who else could it be?—it was much harder to convince myself that he'd be okay if I left him behind and sent help after I'd reached safety.

Sharkey and I emerged from the undergrowth, stepping suddenly onto vegetation-free ground, only to have the earth give way beneath us. I fought to maintain our balance, but Sharkey's broad shoulders and chest made him top-heavy, and he pulled us both over. At least I kept us from pitching forward. Instead we made a slow, sliding tumble to our butts on the soft ground.

Motion on the water caught my eye as we fell. Mike shot to his feet in the canoe, and I had a nightmare vision that he'd forget his bound feet and crack his head open as he vaulted from it. Fortunately, as is usually the case, Mike-in-life showed more common sense than Mike-in-my-head.

"Syd, are you okay?" he shouted, then continued in a voice that strove for casual without quite achieving it. "You look like you've been to a butcher's shop."

I raised a hand in acknowledgment before repeating the agonizing process of getting Sharkey to his feet. "I'm fine. The blood's not mine."

"Come on," Emmett said, giving my ass a nudge with his foot. "Just remember, it still could be."

Mike remained standing as we approached. I'm not sure how he managed it without capsizing the canoe. When we reached the edge of the water, I angled my head free of Sharkey's armpit to hear Emmett's instructions. But there weren't any. My lower back cramped beneath Sharkey's weight.

"Well?" I asked.

"I'm thinking," Emmett said.

Mike swept a long arm toward us, and then took in his own lanky frame. "There's no way we can all fit in this canoe. You need me to paddle, you need that poor guy for—whatever the hell it is that I don't want to know about. And you need you. But you don't need Sydney. Just leave her here."

I appreciated the sentiment, but I didn't think that

option was on the table. And if Emmett ever did leave me behind, I wouldn't bet on it being alive.

Emmett surveyed the scene once more, rubbing his gun shoulder and tilting his head to stretch his neck. I could happily have gone my whole life without witnessing the bad guy version of repetitive stress injury.

"Red," he said, "get him in the canoe with your boyfriend."

I allowed myself a glare, but only mental bird-flipping as Sharkey and I edged closer to the canoe. This time, the freezing water felt good on my feet. I only wished I could dunk the rest of my body, so long as we didn't attract alligators. Sharkey had lost a decent amount of blood, and his face was pale against his dark hair. He stumbled next to Mike's canoe, almost taking both of us down. I grabbed the gunwale to steady myself, and Mike performed some kind of ninja move to maintain his balance and the canoe's. He lowered himself on widely spaced knees.

"Wait," Sharkey said. "I just need a minute to catch my breath."

I'd say he needed a lot more than that, but that's all we could give him at the moment. Mike's face was arm's length from my own, and he took advantage of the lull to quickly lower his sunglasses, enough for me to see his blue-gray eyes. Somehow, the concern and compassion, and even the fear, that I saw there helped firm my own resolve. He slid the glasses back up and gently touched my throat.

"It's not all his blood," Mike said, wiping his fingers on his dark pants before I had a chance to see them.

"All right," Emmett said, standing far enough on shore to keep his feet dry, but close enough to us that he couldn't miss if he pulled the trigger. "Enough of the lovey-dovey. Let's get his ass in the canoe. I'd like to get where we're going before he bleeds out."

Happy thought. But it was true; Sharkey was not looking well. Getting him onboard required an elaborate team effort, with most of his body weight resting upon me while I stood in the river. Mike pulled Sharkey the rest of the way into the vessel just as my legs buckled. I gasped when I was soaked to the waist in the murky, brown water.

"Now would be a good time to do that peeing," Emmett suggested.

I couldn't argue. Mostly because he was pointing a gun at me. He indicated Sharkey's aluminum canoe with the gun.

"Now you get in the shiny one. You'll be my powerhouse." But he couldn't keep a straight face, and snickered as soon as the words left his mouth. *Asshole.*

Sharkey's aluminum canoe sat higher than Mike's, and in slightly deeper water. That meant I had to grab the gunwales and roll in, nearly splitting my lip in the process. Emmett, much closer to Mike's height than my own, had no such difficulties. The canoe wobbled as he stepped in, and he settled in the bow seat facing me.

"You do know this is my first time canoeing?" I asked.

"Yeah, me too. And I don't think I care to repeat the experience." He pulled a cell phone from his pocket and glanced at it. "Shit. Let's get this circus on the road."

You'd think I'd be self-conscious, paddling the canoe while Emmett stared at me, but self-consciousness would have been an indulgence. Instead, I kept one eye on the river ahead of us, one eye on Mike to see how he was approaching the water, and one eye on my own hands and paddle, trying to see how my motions matched up with Mike's. Yes, I know that's one too many eyes. Welcome to my world. No wonder I didn't spare a fourth one for the gun.

The paddling actually wasn't that bad—a mild, straight course with few obstructions—for a while. I was aware of the shoreline passing by without really seeing the details. Trees.

Naked trees. Evergreen trees. Brown water. But then the water began to clear a bit, and things got interesting. The water sped up, which meant we sped up, and the channel narrowed and grew more shallow. I glanced over at Mike, about a canoe length away, and tried not to panic.

"Syd, you've got this," he said. "Just take it nice and slow."

I nodded, as if he could see me, even though he was no doubt watching the water again.

"You think you could put that safety on now," I said to Emmett, more a suggestion than a question.

"No," Emmett said simply. "And don't hit me with the goddamn paddle."

Previously able to ignore him, now I felt Emmett's eyes and gun upon me as the course became more challenging, and that awareness did nothing to help my technique. I began to get dyslexic, either paddling on the wrong side or reversing my letters—pushing when I should have pulled and vice versa.

"Syd!" Mike shouted, if a man can shout calmly. "You need to come back over this way."

"I'm trying," I said. And I was, but the aluminum canoe seemed more persnickety than our plasticky one had, reluctant to respond. And I was distracted by something on the shore, that familiar flash of yellow. My paddle hung in the air as I tried to make sense of what I'd seen.

"Syd!" Mike repeated, less calmly this time. "You need to get away from the shore."

"Hey!" Emmett yelled in my face. "Watch out for the rocks."

I stopped searching for my phantom yellow land sub and saw that they were both right—I needed to take evasive action. I dug my paddle deep into the water and pulled with all my strength... in the wrong direction.

"Are you fucking doing this on purpose?" Emmett screamed.

"Of course I am—yes, I am trying to kill us, and this seemed the most efficient way. What kind of idiot do you think I am!" I screamed back at him.

Although if I'd actually known what I was doing, perilous paddling might not have been a bad strategy.

Ironically, screaming at Emmett helped clear my mind. Something finally clicked, and when I swiveled my hips to paddle on the opposite side, we actually began moving in the right direction. *Huh. Maybe I should scream more often.* I looked over at Mike and smiled. He didn't return my smile, but I could swear his shoulders dropped with relief.

I was still smiling when I turned my attention back to the path ahead of us. And that's when I saw it again in my peripheral vision, a flash in the trees like a yellow flag. It flickered behind tree trunks and shrubs and vines, moving closer to the shore. As was I, unconsciously.

"Hey, dumbass! You're going the wrong way again," Emmett said.

I ignored him and his gun, transfixed by the neon yellow patch. Until finally, finally it broke free.

"It's a dog!" I burst out.

No tail wagging, no happy barking, but it was definitely a canine. Large and muscular, its short hair showed a rich russet on its head and chest and legs where they emerged from a bright yellow jacket. No—a *life* jacket, I realized as the dog bounded over the nearest embankment and launched himself into the river.

Life jacket or not, the dog was working hard. Its rump sank deeper than its dramatically kicking front end as it swam toward the canoes. I quickly surveyed the course of the river, and the people on it. More rocks lay ahead, and Mike's attention alternated between those and Emmett and me in the aluminum canoe. Sitting in front of Mike, Sharkey was hunched over and avoided looking at the dog.

Because it's Sharkey's dog, I realized. And his dog had probably been watching Mike and me from the shore back at the spring. Was he looking for his owner then as well?

My eyes finally came to rest on Emmett in the bow. He was watching the dog, and where his eyes went his gun followed. It was stupid—there was a good chance the man would kill all of us—but the thought of him shooting a swimming dog triggered incredible anger and revulsion in me.

"Hey! What are you doing?" I yelled.

"What do you think I'm doing? I'm not gonna let that goddamn dog eat me!" But his gun swung back toward me as he said it.

My arms froze instinctively, which meant my paddle stopped midair. I waited, breathless, for Emmett to point the gun elsewhere and for my senses to return to me, along with my ability to move. But Emmett simply glared at me, as if the sweat soaking the neck of his shirt, as if the dog swimming toward us, as if *everything* that brought him to hijack a canoe on a north Florida river, was *my* fault.

Emmett's mouth opened, and I anticipated—what? His justification for shooting me? An angry guttural sound before a bullet traveled five feet or so to enter my chest? Every scenario ended with a bullet. His silence dragged and my apprehension grew by the nanosecond, until...

With me too distracted/terrified to steer it, our canoe went where the current directed it. Right into a rock. The bow slammed against the unyielding surface, my body lurched forward, and I nearly dropped my paddle.

And Emmett pulled the trigger.

10

I gasped and looked down in a panic, my paddle smacking against the canoe as I clutched my midsection. But I wasn't bleeding, at least no more than I had been before.

I may not have been shot, but the canoe wasn't so lucky. Water poured into the hull through a dime-sized hole at a rate comparable to my wide-open kitchen faucet.

"Sonofabitch!" Emmett said, looking from the gun in his hand to the punctured canoe hull. "Shit!"

"Syd, are you okay?" Mike yelled.

I nodded, but my ears were still ringing and I couldn't find words. Sure, I was grateful that I wasn't the one leaking, but it was too surreal, watching our vessel fill up with water while a man still held a gun pointed in my general direction. Minus only one bullet, with a few more to go.

"Fuck!" Emmett continued, lifting his feet gingerly as though his sneakers would dissolve in liquid.

"The canoe won't sink," Sharkey said.

"That's easy for you to say, sitting in the goddamn dry

one," snapped the man who'd shot a hole in a formerly dry one.

"It won't," Sharkey reassured him, voice weak and cracking with the effort. "You can't see them, but there are flotation tanks in the ends. It might get uncomfortable, but I promise it will not sink."

"It will get more difficult to paddle, as it fills and submerges," Mike said. "That's an extra eight pounds of weight for every gallon of water. Sydney and I should switch canoes. She's a novice, and it'd be easier for her to handle this one."

"You'd like that, wouldn't you?" Emmett yelled, now waving the gun toward Mike. "Just shut the fuck up and let me think for a minute."

I dipped my paddle gently back into the water, using steady, deliberate motions, not wanting to antagonize the man but not wanting us to ram anything else either. Who knew what he'd shoot the next time? At least the dog had shown good sense, swimming back to shore. He climbed the gentle bank and shook himself vigorously, then stood with head and tail held high, before resuming a course parallel to ours on dry land. It was easy to track his yellow vest, now that I knew what it was. Or what it was supposed to be...

I've seen a fair number of embarrassed-looking canines in flotation devices on St. George Island's dog-friendly beaches, and this dog's vest hadn't floated right. Was its purpose something other than buoyancy—storage, perhaps? Of whatever Emmett was searching for, whatever it was that he thought Sharkey had. What better place to hide... I didn't know, but when in doubt, drugs... than in the lining of a big dog's life vest?

No wonder Sharkey hadn't called the dog to him. Whoever Emmett worked for only needed Sharkey as long as they didn't know where he'd stashed their stuff. With that information, their cost-benefit analysis might suggest they kill Sharkey, and any other loose ends (aka us). Unless they wanted the man around to make an example of him. Maybe they'd just give Sharkey a stern talking-to. I looked at the water bubbling into the hull, the bullet hole invisible beneath it. Yeah, right, they'd go all suburban mom on Sharkey's ass. With Mike and me right there for the finger-wagging.

"Give me your shirt!" Emmett barked.

Despite being the only other person in the canoe, I was slow to realize he was talking to me. Although I was wearing a bikini top under my shirt, I didn't want to survive a maniac with a gun just to succumb to sun poisoning. "You have a shirt you're not using," I countered.

Emmett pointed, with a finger in addition to the gun, indicating he wouldn't soon forget my behavior, but reached for his unworn flannel shirt. He tried to jam a bit of sleeve into the hole one-handed, but the shirt kept floating and spreading, blocking his view. And the water kept pouring in. Emmett growled a noise of frustration before flinging the wet shirt at me. It spattered water across my sunglasses and onto my pants.

"Fix it!"

It would take a helluva lot more than a smelly man's flannel shirt to fix this situation. Or maybe not...

I kneeled in the growing puddle of water in the hull, my shins turning to ice. The canoe wobbled, but Emmett could hardly complain. It rocked even more as I pushed the heavy, cheap fabric against the water flow. Suddenly I jerked my hand back, out of the water, as though I'd cut my finger.

"Sonofabitch!" I yelled. I clutched my hand to me, hissing, and said, "Great. I'll be lucky if I don't lose my goddamn finger in this dirty water."

"You won't be breathing long enough to lose your finger, if you don't plug that goddamned hole," Emmett said.

I didn't discount his threat, but the water filling the hull was obviously making him nervous. I shook out my hand again before returning to my task, imitating Emmett's prior one-handed efforts as I held the supposedly injured hand at chest height.

"It won't stay. I need more leverage to push the shirt through," I said, raising my knee on the same side.

The canoe shifted, warning that we were leaving the neighborhood of initial stability behind. But the vessel didn't shift as much as I'd hoped, probably because of the rising water level inside the canoe.

"What the hell are you doing?" Emmett asked.

He leaned for a closer look; I'd never have a better opportunity. I grabbed the gunwale with my faux injured hand and jerked it toward me as I pressed down on the other side. We rocked, but it wasn't enough. At least, not until Emmett panicked and overbalanced, waving his arms in the air to compensate. And then, in one great lurch, the canoe capsized.

My body clenched all over against the sudden slap of cold water, and a rushing, bubbling sound filled my ears as I went under and stayed there. I opened my eyes, and saw a dark shape I assumed was Emmett. I reached above me, shoved the canoe toward him and felt a satisfying thump. But where was his gun? I couldn't have seen a neon green bazooka in the tannic water.

My safest bet was to stay submerged as long as possible. The water was over my head, but not by much, and I stayed mostly upright as the current carried me downstream. I tried to keep the fingertips of one hand against the canoe for reference, but it began swinging around in the current when we hit an eddy.

Finally, short of breath and with Emmett's silhouette nowhere to be seen, I surfaced to the sound of Mike calling my name. Streaming water blurred my eyesight and I wasn't sure where his voice was coming from. I held both hands as high in the air as I could, giving a double thumbs-up, before submerging again briefly to sweep my long, tangled hair out of my face. I hadn't heard any gunshots and figured if Emmett were pointing a gun at me, he'd be yelling or Mike would be warning me. Although maybe that's why Mike had been yelling. Pressing the water from my face and blinking it from my lashes, I turned in a slow circle, lungs full and ready to duck.

The damaged aluminum canoe floated upside down a few yards away. Mike's intact one shot toward me like a torpedo, veering at the last moment to pass alongside instead of mowing me down. Mike held out an arm, but I shook my head.

"Where's Emmett?" I asked, treading water. So long as I kept moving, I wouldn't turn into an ice cube.

"I don't know," Mike said. "I lost him, trying to keep an eye on you."

"I'll get the other canoe."

I swam to it easily and found the water shallow enough to stand. Mike paddled next to me, Sharkey still pale and silent. I left the canoe upside down but grabbed the bow line (or was it the stern?) and asked, "What do you think?"

Mike gazed first downstream, then at the shore to our right. "We can haul it out and leave it. Or—wait, what's that over there?"

I scanned the tree-lined shore where he'd pointed, shading my eyes with my hand. I must have lost my sunglasses in the river. An unnatural slice of white caught my attention, the edge of a sneaker sole's trim gleaming like a whitewall tire. A shape I'd taken for an alligator hauling out was, on closer examination, an unmoving human leg. I looked at Mike, and suddenly we were in motion together. He stepped easily out of the intact canoe while I handed Sharkey the damaged one's line. Mike matched his longer stride to mine as we sloshed toward the body through increasingly shallow water.

"Remember," Mike said, pausing about ten yards from the shape on the ground, "he may still have a gun."

Yeah, no danger of me forgetting that. "Split up, and you approach from the left, me from the right?"

Mouth set in a twisted line, Mike did not look happy.

"You got a better idea?" I asked.

"No," he admitted. "And two targets are better than one. I just hate sentences that involve us as the word 'targets.'"

I couldn't disagree.

Near shore, the water diminished to knee-high but was murky, and I walked cautiously to avoid turning an ankle. The riverbank was low—no more than a high step—but I stumbled when it collapsed beneath me. The soil, a poorly mixed reddish brown compost with dark gray chunks and sandy white grains, stuck to my knees. I brushed the dirt off while I waited for Mike to maneuver into position on the other side.

I approached the motionless body, barely visible through some kind of leafy, evergreen branches. What if Emmett was dead? I wouldn't exactly mourn for the guy, but could we really leave his body out here to rot or be gnawed upon? I thought about Mike's bloody friend in the canoe, and about a ruined first date that—let's face it—I'd hoped would be more "meet-cute" than "meet psycho."

Yes, I decided, I could definitely leave Emmett's dead body out here to rot.

Mike and I had nearly closed the gap between us when

the body moved. Emmett's legs wiggled, and he scrambled deeper into the brush on his elbows. Or at least, he tried. Mike was faster, grabbing both his legs just above the ankles. Emmett howled as Mike dragged him out.

"Oh, God, my leg!" Emmett yelled. "Please, stop!"

Mike released his legs and Emmett rolled onto his side, groaning.

"Well, I guess we don't have to worry about him running," Mike said.

I looked down at the writhing man. I didn't see any bones sticking out, but it would take quite a catastrophic injury for them to poke through his jeans. One leg curled, and Emmett's hands hovered over it, not quite touching, while the other leg alternated between straightening and slow kicking. It didn't take a doctor to figure out which one he'd injured.

"High or low?" I asked, bending over him.

"It's my knee," Emmett moaned, clutching his hands to the back of his head. "It's my goddamned knee."

"Where's your gun?" Mike asked. Not waiting for a response, he ran his hands over Emmett, searching for a weapon. The only thing he found was a pocketknife, the one Sharkey had held to my throat. I decided against mentioning that now, and Mike slipped it into his own pocket before stating the obvious. "No cell phone, either."

"Do you think I'd be laying here, having a conversation with you, if I still had my cell phone? Or my gun?" Emmett said.

"Come on," Mike said, dragging Emmett out of the brush by his shoulders. Mike stopped when he reached a clear area of shore, dropping the man's upper body to the ground. "You okay staying with him while I bring Sharkey in?" Mike asked.

I stared at Emmett but, groaning in pain, he seemed senseless to our conversation.

"Fine," I said, and raised my voice in the hopes that Emmett would hear me. "If he gives me any trouble, I'll break his other goddamn knee."

Something about the man had awakened a dark, predatory part of me, and I meant every word.

11

———

"Jesus," Emmett moaned, "I need something for the pain."

"Oh yeah?" I asked, watching Mike pull both canoes toward shore, Sharkey clutching the gunwales of the properly floating one. "How about a rock upside your head? 'Cause that's all I've got."

He stopped talking, but kept writhing. At least that prevented him from freaking out when the yellow-vested dog appeared as Mike helped Sharkey onto dry land. Mike supported his friend on one side, and the big animal walked on the other, pressed against the outfitter as though to break his fall. Once Sharkey was settled, Mike approached me and Emmett, carrying the nylon strap that had earlier secured his own feet in the canoe. He looped it around Emmett's hands in a pattern that escaped me, then cinched it quickly, eliciting a yelp from Emmett. Mike loosened it a hair, then nodded for me to follow him. He hadn't spoken a word.

Sharkey lay on the ground out of Emmett's hearing range, especially in Emmett's current condition. Sharkey's upper body rested against a large, rounded rock, and the dog sat next to him.

"In case you haven't guessed," Mike said, "this is Sydney. Syd, this is Levi Sharkey."

Sharkey tipped his hat, then nodded toward the dog. "And that's Meathead. Don't ask—he came with the name."

"He doesn't talk much," I said, rubbing the top of the animal's head. He tolerated the attention, eventually half-closing one eye as my hand crawled to the side of his face and scratched at his jaw.

"Rhodesian ridgeback," Sharkey said. "They tend not to waste their breath. Unlike the rest of us."

I remained standing—ostensibly because it made it easier to keep an eye on Emmett—while Mike sat next to Sharkey. Adrenaline hummed through my body. I tried to ride it out by scratching the dog's face bald on one side. I wanted to hate the man who'd messed up our day so monumentally, but it was hard to hate a man with a dog.

"How are you holding up?" I asked.

"I'll live," Sharkey said. "I'm in better shape than my canoe."

Unable to interpret his tone, my eyes narrowed. Dog owner shine only goes so far. "I hope you're not blaming me for that."

"No," Sharkey said, lifting a bloody finger. "But you are the one who grabbed me—"

"While being held at gunpoint," I said, forcefully enough for the dog to leave me and cross to Mike's other side.

Mike's voice was strained when he said, "Look, we need to calm down and put our heads together—"

"You didn't tell me that!" Sharkey protested.

"Kinda hard to do when you're trying to slit my throat!" I should have let it go, but I couldn't help it—that one still pissed me off. Not to mention it stung a little too, now that I was out of the bacteria-laden water.

"He did what?" Mike demanded, looking from me to Sharkey and back to me. His neck tensed and his shoulders went rigid.

I've seen Mad Mike so rarely, I'd forgotten that he's someone we probably didn't want to see again. At least, not until we had a clear idea where to point him. As is often the case, the need to defuse someone else's temper helped curb my own.

I said, "So why don't you tell us what the hell's going on, and then we can decide who's justified being pissed off at whom?"

Sharkey's face screwed up on one side while Mike continued to glare at him. "You warned me she has a way with words." He took a moment to catch his breath before raising one hand in contrition, the other still clutching his bloody side. "I'm sorry. I'm not blaming you for any of this. Hell, if I were going to blame anybody, it'd be Leonard."

"The kid who works for you?" Mike asked.

"You've met him?" Sharkey sighed and shook his head. The man's color was not good, a gray that brought to mind the hull of his aluminum canoe, now resting upside down in the shade. "Leonard is a good kid."

"Oh, come on, Levi!" Mike snapped, hand straying to his forehead as though his hat were the only thing keeping him from yanking his own hair out.

"I'll bet you wouldn't have rolled your eyes if people had said that about you when you were his age," Sharkey said.

I looked at the man, trying to figure out how old he was (mid-thirties, no older than Mike), what he knew about Mike that I didn't, and how he knew it. But before I could go too far down that rabbit hole, Sharkey continued. Lately, Leonard had been tardy for work, distracted while he was there, and had generally acted "off."

"How lately is lately?" I asked.

"The past few months," Sharkey said. "I figured it was because he'd made the college stuff official, and it was just—you know—a transition thing."

I heard a hint of New York in Sharkey's voice, buried deep but coming out during a time of extreme stress. He cleared his throat carefully before continuing. "I talked to him. Leonard apologized and said everything was fine. But he would, with his cousin there. Leonard had some minor trouble at school a couple of years ago, and Ken's ridden him hard since then. Anyway, last week, I caught Leonard on his cell phone out by the canoe racks. I didn't get details, but I heard enough to know he was in some kind of trouble. I confronted him; he denied it."

Mike ran his hand in a circle, motioning for him to move it along.

Sharkey swallowed, mouth dry. "Finally, last night, I had to go back for something I'd left at the office. What do I find, but someone smacking the shit out of Leonard in the parking lot."

"He didn't look that bad today," I said. Although the head-lowering I'd assumed was shyness could have another explanation.

"I said smacking, not beating. Mostly open-handed, and they took off when I showed up. I don't think they'd been at it very long."

"They?" Mike asked.

"Couple of guys." Sharkey jerked a thumb toward Emmett, curled in a ball. "Like this guy, but not him. So I ask Leonard what the hell's going on, and this time he's scared enough to tell me. Leonard's been using my business to run drugs."

"How?" Mike asked.

"Somebody approached him late last year, said he knew Leonard needed some money, and all he had to do was pass a friend a package. The friend would show up for one of our tours, say something special, and they'd do the exchange. *Technically*, Leonard didn't know what was in the package—he never looked inside. He didn't know any of the people by name, and he never recognized them, so they couldn't have been too local."

Mike stood, looked out at the water, and began pacing, wearing a shallow trench in the sandy ground.

"How many times did he do this?" I asked.

"Two or three," Sharkey said. "Once a month. But like I said, Leonard's a good kid who made a bad decision. This last time, he said he was done, that he didn't want to have anything else to do with them."

"And 'they' came by last night to let him know that wasn't an option," I concluded.

Sharkey nodded and closed his eyes.

"You have any water?" I asked.

He looked at his empty, upside-down canoe, and then out at the river. "I used to," Sharkey said.

I sidestepped Mike as I walked to the other canoe and retrieved my water bottle. "Don't mind my cooties," I said, handing it to Sharkey.

"Thanks," he said, sipping conservatively.

I wanted to tell him to drink the whole damn thing, but until I took stock of our supply—and until we decided our course of action—I was afraid we might need to ration it. And we definitely needed to get Sharkey medical attention. Mike's pacing was wearing through my last nerve, so I stuck out an arm to stop him when he came close.

"Sorry," he said, and turned back to Sharkey. "You didn't call the cops?"

Rueful, Sharkey shook his head. If nothing else, his injuries seemed to have helped him recognize his folly of the past twenty-four hours. "I didn't even tell Ken. Leonard begged me not to, and I guess I didn't have a sense of the scale of what I was getting into. They'd left a package with Leonard. He had a burner number for somebody, so I called and said Leonard was out of it. He wasn't passing on the package, but he wasn't turning them in, either. He just wanted to walk away. And as a show of good faith, he'd return the package."

Mike stared down at his friend. He pulled off his hat and raked a hand through his hair. "Dammit, Levi, how could you be so stupid? Let me guess... you set up a meet, but this morning they called to change it."

Sharkey's eyes kept drifting shut, and he either wasn't aware of it or was too exhausted and in too much pain to care. "I didn't want Leonard to go because I didn't think it was safe."

"But you, *you* can handle anything," Mike said. "And now here we all are, paying for your goddamned arrogance."

I think he'd hoped to provoke the man, but Sharkey simply met his friend's scowl and said, "Yes. I'm sorry, Mike."

I cut in, weary of their bromantic conflict. "I assume you met the men at the launch where we found your vehicle. How many were there?"

"Two," he said. "I showed up early and had the canoe in the water and Meathead in the canoe before they showed."

I walked to the ignobly named dog and traced his big skull with my fingers. By some sort of magical transference, it stimulated my own brain. "Because you'd changed your mind," I said. "While you were waiting, you decided you weren't going to give them the package after all."

Sharkey didn't contradict me. Note to self: blood loss (the

other party's, not your own) is a great tool for winning argu-
ments and interrogations. "Why didn't you just leave?"

"I was afraid if I didn't show up at all, they'd get to
Leonard before I could. And I'd hoped I could buy us some
time to figure out a real solution."

I stretched to give Meathead a good pat all the way down
the length of his back. The padding felt different toward the
rear of his vest, and I smacked it with my palm. "That's when
you put the package in Meathead's life vest."

Sharkey's   head   tilted   with   interest.   "Not   just   a
pretty face."

"That's right," I said. "I have fabulous hair, too." A statement which was complete bravado—I was sure I had nothing
of the sort, but rather my usual north Florida coiffure, a damp
mass of frizz. I bent for a closer look at the flotation device,
curious how he'd managed the clandestine operation under
the gun. So to speak.

Sharkey watched my scrutiny. "Meathead tore up his vest
once, and I'd replaced the floaty bit myself and secured it
with Velcro. Made this simple."

"How'd you get the knife wound?" Mike asked, pointing.
"It is a knife wound, isn't it?"

"It was the second guy, not the one that was with you,"
Sharkey said. "I don't think he even planned to; things just
got out of hand. They were searching my car, he had the knife
out, I ran for the canoe..."

"Puncture or slice?" Mike asked, moving toward him.

Sharkey waved him away. "Just a flesh wound," he said,
trying to smile but grimacing instead. "It's not bleeding
anymore."

Probably because he was out of blood.

"I swear I took a look at it," Sharkey said. "And remember,
I'm First Aid certified."

"Certifiable is more like it," Mike muttered, putting his

hat back on and pulling it down snug. "Fine. We have to assume the knife guy is waiting for you—waiting for us—downriver. Presumably at your dock. You guys open today?"

Sharkey straightened, wincing. "Yeah, but you're the only person we had booked, and we rarely get foot traffic out of season. You think they went inside? You think they got Leonard? And Ken?"

Mike leaned back, looking up at the sky. Which is much closer to his face than to mine.

"*They* didn't," I said, working through the possibilities out loud, "because Emmett stayed behind to deal with you and ruin our day. So with just one guy, there's a good chance he's sitting in the parking lot. Or if he went in, he hasn't done anything yet. He can't assume no customers will come in to complicate things."

"But what happens if we don't show up? If his partner doesn't show up?" Sharkey asked.

Mike looked at me, face static and expression blank, but I knew what he was thinking. And he was waiting for me to say it out loud, so he didn't have to. That told me he and Sharkey were more than casual acquaintances.

"Guys?" Sharkey prompted. "What happens?"

But I wasn't ready to voice my own concerns explicitly, for the sake of Sharkey's mental state or my own. Instead I said, "Nothing good, for us or your employees. We need a plan."

12

"Your friend doesn't look good."

"I know," Mike acknowledged as we pushed the remaining river-worthy canoe far enough from the shore to keep it from bottoming out when we got in. We'd decided our only option was to paddle to Sharkey's place and take our chances.

"Anything strike you as weird about his story?" I asked.

"Specifically?"

"I don't know. I don't know the man, but something just feels off. Why would anyone use *his* business as a cover?"

Mike stretched out his arms, rotated them in a few broad circles, then tugged on his shirt at the neckline to straighten it. I tried to not be distracted by the way it clung to one muscled shoulder.

"Lots of tourists, so people coming in from out of town aren't suspicious?" he speculated. "Maybe it's not about Levi's business. Maybe it's about Leonard, and he just happens to work for Levi."

"Maybe," I said, shading my eyes against the bright sky.

Mike reached into the canoe and pulled out my now-wet Red Sox cap with a flourish, albeit a token one. "I'm afraid your sunglasses are long gone, but I thought you might want this," he said, settling it on my head and tucking my hair behind my ears. "Now that they've finally won a World Series."

My attachment to the item had less to do with my favorite team and more to do with how I'd acquired it, as a gift from Mike when I'd landed in the hospital not long after we met. "Thank you," I said, and leaned in, noticing that his clothes were entirely too dry. That would be easy to fix, as wet as mine still were...

"Mike!" Sharkey yelled.

Mike and I spun to find his friend was fine, but our prisoner was making a break for it. Emmett had freed his hands and was dragging himself toward the cover of the forest. I had a step's advantage on Mike as we dashed clumsily through the shallow water, until I heard a curse, followed by a great splash, behind me.

No worries—if I couldn't apprehend a man with one functional leg by myself, Glenn would have my ass. Assuming I lived to tell him about it. I was panting by the time I hit dry land, but caught up with Emmett within a few strides. That's when I realized I hadn't really thought through how to stop him. Fall on top of the man?

"Hey, asshole!" I yelled, thinking he might just roll over and give up.

He didn't. Instead, he swung his arm in a wild arc as I crouched over him, metal glinting in his hand. He missed, and I kicked his injured leg. Shrieking, Emmett curled into a ball, still holding a knife. I stepped on his arm—as he had with Sharkey—and bent to grab the weapon from his slackened fingers. A folding knife with a matte black blade, it wasn't especially long, but it was bigger than Sharkey's pock-etknife, and purely intended to do damage rather than open the occasional bottle of beer or piece of junk mail.

"How the hell did I miss that?" Mike gasped next to me, now dripping wet to his mid-chest.

I shrugged, still short of breath, and the motion reminded me I was standing on Emmett's arm. It seemed like a good place to be. I stuffed the knife in the back of my snug tights. "You see the strap?" I asked.

Mike found its remains quickly enough a few feet away. Emmett had sliced through the binding, but the strap was long and there was plenty left to restrain him. Mike secured his hands (Emmett was still whimpering, in too much pain to protest) and gathered up the remaining lengths of nylon.

"How do you want to carry him?" I asked.

Mike stood, one hand on his hip and the other rubbing his square chin. "I don't think it matters. No matter what, it's gonna hurt like hell," Mike said, then bent to slip his hands beneath Emmett's shoulders. "Good thing I don't care."

"Oh sure, leave me with the kicky end," I said, cupping my hands beneath Emmett's calves. His groans took on a teeth-grinding quality, but he didn't scream. We nearly dropped him twice (did I mention how hard it is to walk backwards while carrying a redneck?), but eventually made our awkward, splashing way to the canoe.

Mike and I stood, Emmett hanging between us, and Mike said, "On three."

I shook my head, breathless and punchy, and said, "I hate that counting crap. Are we swinging him like a bag of garbage, or just dropping him inside?"

"I don't think you can lift him high enough, so let's go for garbage," Mike said.

I swung too soon, and Emmett's feet banged in the hull

half a second before the rest of his body, creating an almost syncopated sound that he ruined with a yelp.

"Crazy bitch!" Emmett yelled, while Mike moved our bag in the canoe.

Emmett had lost his hat, and he squinted against the bright sky as I bent over him. I seized his wet, greasy hair. He grunted as I raised his head and said, "That's right. It's Crazy Bitch. Not Red. And don't you forget it."

And then I dropped his head to the hull, before I could bang it against the bottom, over and over. I gripped the gunwale to help me resist the temptation.

A light tremor ran through my limbs. My blood sugar was getting low, and I am the first person to admit I am a damned cranky hungry person, the type of person *hangry* was coined for (or more like, about). It made it hard to think straight.

That's what I told myself. That I was hangry, not a sociopath.

"Syd!" Mike said, tossing a protein bar at me, as if he'd read my mind.

My gratitude was somewhat hampered by his wonky throw—I nearly dropped the chalky nugget in the river—but I lifted the bar in acknowledgement. "Thanks."

"We've got a lot of paddling to do," he said, pulling pieces of strap from his pockets and securing one of Emmett's feet to the yoke. "And I can hear your stomach."

"How much paddling?" I asked, wishing I had my water bottle and trying not to choke to death on the protein bar. It was like chewing a lightly flavored desiccant pack.

"Levi will know," Mike said, sipping from a water bottle while he stared down at Emmett. "The real question is what's waiting for us when we get there."

I handed Mike half the protein bar and he passed me his water bottle. He was right; so far we'd made a lot of educated guesses about whether we'd be shot on sight, and if so, by

whom. Between us, we'd investigated a fair number of criminal cases, albeit from the defense point of view, so our
guesses were a little more educated than the Average Jane and
Joe. But when it came down to it, neither of us was exactly a
criminal mastermind. Of course, it didn't sound like this
bunch was either, if they were recruiting high school seniors.

"Is your partner waiting for us?" I asked, pointing the
water bottle at Emmett with hands that still showed a
modest quiver.

He twisted his head to stare at the opposite shore, silent.
Almost without thinking, I pressed the bottle against the top
edge of his kneecap.

"Mother fucker!" Emmett squealed, bound hands flailing.

"Where is he?" I asked, releasing the pressure. "Where's
your buddy?"

"He's at the canoe place, like you said," Emmett said,
through gritted teeth.

"Alone?" I asked.

"Fuck you."

I set the water bottle in the canoe, out of range of
Emmett's thrashing, and reached behind my back for the
knife I'd taken from him. His eyes stretched wide and he
started to shiver beneath his sweat. I concentrated on
keeping my hands steady while I searched for a notch in the
blade with wet, soft fingernails, only to have my thumb
fumble over a protruding stud instead. My vision swam, and
in place of the knife by the river I saw bolt cutters in a dim
storage unit.

Lost in that phantom image, my heart skipped when
Mike's long-fingered hand (*all ten fingers intact*) materialized
next to my own. I glanced at him as I placed the knife on his
open, waiting palm, but his reflective sunglasses didn't meet
my gaze.

"Is he alone?" Mike asked. The blade stayed hidden as he

pressed the hilt of the knife against the edge of Emmett's knee, much as I had with the water bottle. Just more effectively, and painfully.

"Yes!" Emmett screeched. "He's alone!"

The canoe rocked as Mike eased off the knife's pressure. "And what's he doing there?"

Breathing heavily, Emmett's voice was close to a sob. "Waiting in the parking lot. I'm supposed to let him know when we get close, but he's watching for canoes to come in to the dock. Anybody that shows up, he'll grab before they can get inside."

"How long will he wait?" I asked.

"I don't know."

Mike jammed the hilt against his kneecap again.

"I don't know!" Emmett shrieked. "But if it's too long, he'll just take the kid."

"Leonard?" Mike asked.

"Yeah. Leonard."

Mike stepped away from the canoe and wiped the sweat from his upper lip with his forearm. My own face was flushed with heat, while my submerged calves were freezing. My stomach churned and I felt as though I was going to throw up. Emmett looked much the same.

"Will he kill the kid?" I asked.

"I don't know," Emmett muttered, clutching his bound hands and hugging his elbows to his torso. "Maybe. But at the very least I sure as hell won't be the only one walking with a limp."

I sloshed to where Mike stood, staring at Sharkey, who was lying near the beached, damaged canoe. Meathead's vest was the only spot of color near the ashen man.

"We need to go," Mike said. "Now."

No way would we all fit in the solid canoe with Emmett, and I could barely maneuver the aluminum canoe before

Emmett shot a hole in it. "Can you handle the 'colander canoe' with Sharkey?" I asked, hating for Mike to do it but knowing it was our only chance.

I heard the same assessment in his voice when he replied, "I guess I'll have to."

——————

13

Mike retrieved the damaged canoe while I saw to our wounded passenger—the one we hadn't wounded ourselves, that is. Meathead sat upright and Sharkey lifted his head as I approached. My brows wrinkled when he swatted feebly at a few flies that circled his bloody abdomen.

"If I didn't know better, I'd think you were worried about me," he croaked.

"The only thing I'm worried about is whether I'll have to fight Mike for your dog when you die," I said, rubbing the ridgeback's ears. It sounded harsher out loud than it had in my head. I gave Meathead one last pat and turned to Sharkey. "Sorry—was that too much?"

Sharkey's lips had faded to match his gray face, and his eyes were rimmed with red. "He likes yogurt, but it makes him fart. Don't give him more than a spoonful, or you'll regret it."

"I'll try to remember that," I said, as Mike joined us.

"How far is it to your place?" Mike asked.

"Maybe three miles."

"So that's what, an hour of paddling?" Mike guessed.

"With you paddling, or me?" Sharkey cracked a half smile.

"Me paddling the two of us in a sinking canoe," Mike replied.

Sharkey's smile faded. "You might be able to do it in an hour."

Mike helped Sharkey stand, and I rushed to steady the swaying man from the other side. I could feel his legs shaking as he leaned heavily against us on the way to the canoes.

"The canoe's gonna get unstable as it fills. We'll need to empty it from time to time," Sharkey said, short of breath. "Fortunately, the river is fairly shallow from here to my place, and you're the Jolly Green Giant—"

Mike managed a ghost of a smile, as though that were a running joke with his shorter friend. "So I ought to be able to handle it."

I was certain Mike already had something in mind, but when we reached the water, I lowered my voice to ask, "What happens when we get there? We can't just go rolling in with no real weapons, two injured people, and a sinking canoe."

"I was thinking," Mike began cautiously, as though anticipating my objection, "we'd pull over before we get to the dock and leave you on shore."

I considered our options while I adjusted my grip on Sharkey's arm. His other one was draped over Mike, but the arm on his injured side was too painful to raise. There weren't many options, and we were almost to the canoe, so my deliberation didn't take long.

"Okay," I said. "That sounds good."

Mike didn't reply. I guessed he was either too shocked or afraid to say anything that might change my mind.

I continued, "Then I'll run over to Sharkey's place and scope it out before you guys get there."

Sharkey grunted when Mike straightened, no doubt trying

to use his height advantage. "Sydney——" Mike began, but I cut him off.

"It makes sense. This guy has never seen me, and we agreed he won't want to draw any unwanted attention by harassing a random customer. I can come up with a story for why I'm there."

"Syd, I have every confidence in your ability to come up with something. But what happens when Leonard..." Mike's voice trailed off, perhaps searching for words that didn't sound like they'd come from a primetime crime drama. Unsuccessfully. "... When he blows your cover?"

"He won't," I said, with much more confidence than I felt.

Lifting a paddle wasn't easy after we'd muscled Emmett and Sharkey into canoes, but I didn't have a choice. Mike set off, long arms and paddle working together to make ridiculously expansive strokes, but I took a moment to free Emmett's leg before following. Mike had used some kind of fancy sailor's knot that would undoubtedly release instantly for him, but less so for me. Lips pursed, focused on my frustrating task, I still caught a glimpse of cunning on Emmett's face. Hands bound, knee blown out, not the sharpest pencil in the drawer... And yet, it would be foolish to underestimate the man. That's one reason I hadn't objected to Meathead joining us in the canoe.

Once we were underway, the dog was so calm and still he could have been a sculpture in the bow, save for his nose occasionally drifting in an odd direction, dragged by a novel smell. I didn't have much of an eye for the passing scenery, playing what-if in my head instead. What would I have done with Emmett's knife if it had instantly opened? And—almost as important—what did Mike think I would have done? What would either of us have done if Emmett hadn't answered our questions? We already seemed unwilling or unable to look at each other. Would that change when we got out of this? *If* we got out of this... What if Emmett was wrong about how many people were waiting for us? And what if his partner decided to shoot first and ask questions later?

My inadequate paddling skills did provide some relief from my obsessing brain. Anytime my concentration lapsed, the tandem tried to make a break for the shore or for Mike's gradually sinking canoe. I wondered if Mike had a cutoff depth for water in the hull, or maybe he'd use regular time intervals. Emmett's shirtsleeve (wedged in the hole before setting out) kept the river from pouring in, but it still accumulated pretty quickly.

The first time Mike stopped to jettison water was in a shallow area (shin deep for him, but close to Sharkey's knees) without a strong current. Unable to park (having not been introduced to the canoe brakes), I drifted slowly past as Mike disembarked before helping Sharkey painfully roll out. Flipping the canoe didn't seem to take much effort, but when Mike levered it free of the river before setting it back down, I suspected he'd be unable to stand tomorrow.

The second time he dumped the canoe, I was sure of it.

Mike had just dumped the canoe a third time when I heard a car in the not-so-distant distance. It made sense that we were getting near the highway. Sharkey's riverside business had also been close to the highway, ergo, we must be getting closer to Sharkey's as well. And none too soon. Aching arms and shoulders were bad enough, but my hands sported raised blisters that were eager to pop.

Ahead of us, the river made a grand but gradual bend to the right. Sharkey pointed at the shore on the left side as he and Mike swung in that direction. After a short, unintended jaunt to the right (paddle dyslexia relapse), I followed. They hauled in alongside an embankment with a rare, modest rise, choked by shrubby growth and intermittent, scraggly conifers. Emmett had been quiet, but he grunted a protest and ensured his limbs were in the center of our canoe as we bumped against Sharkey's aluminum one. Meathead glanced at Emmett, and the man fell silent again.

"Is that the highway up there?" I asked, thinking the embankment had been built up to accommodate it.

"Yes," Sharkey said. "And the turn for my place is maybe a couple hundred yards ahead."

With vegetation growing nearly to the edge of the bank, there was no room to beach the canoes. Mike helped Sharkey step into the water (thigh-deep on the shorter man this time) before securing the vessel's lines to something. I didn't see what, too busy fighting a feeling of panic when I rolled into the water (on purpose) and felt my feet sinking in the bottom (not so much). It couldn't have been more than a couple of inches, but it was still creepy. Trying to pull a foot loose from the powerful bottom suction, I fell sideways and submerged to my ears before Mike caught me. Hands around my ribs, he lifted me free and set me on my feet.

I coughed and wiped the water from my face with wet hands. "Thanks," I said.

Mike's hands rested on my hips. It was our first real physical contact since Emmett's Tarantino-style interrogation. "Syd, are you sure about this?"

I nodded. "Leonard's just a kid. If there's any way we can get him out of this in one piece..."

"You're not going to call the cops, are you?" Sharkey demanded. "The last thing the kid needs is for the authorities to get involved."

I high-stepped carefully through the muck toward the injured man, even though it meant disengaging from Mike. "I'll give you a blood loss freebie for saying something so stupid. Of course I'm going to call the cops! There is no end to this for Leonard unless the authorities are involved. I know you don't want to see his future messed up, but let's make sure Leonard *has* a future first."

Mike gripped my shoulder from behind, a gentle reminder to soften toward his friend. After all, Sharkey hadn't intended to mess up our day. He'd been trying to do the right thing. He couldn't help it he was an idiot out of his depth.

"Look, I know a good lawyer if he needs one. The kid'll be okay," I reassured Sharkey. Then I asked Mike, "You need help with this bit? Playing musical canoe chairs, I mean?"

"No, I think I've got it," he said. "You should get moving if you want to get there ahead of us."

Mike was right, but I couldn't help feeling I was forgetting something. "Has the other guy seen Meathead?"

Sharkey chewed on his dry, bottom lip. "I'm not sure," he admitted. "Meathead was waiting for me in the canoe, so he never got a *close* look at the dog."

"Good enough. I'll take him with me; you'd be a little crowded with the dog in tow. And you'll be safer if he's not with you," I said, unwilling to be more explicit in front of Emmett. I figured no matter what happened when they arrived at the dock, Mike and Sharkey—and even Leonard— had a better chance of survival so long as the location of the package (currently strapped to Meathead) was still in play.

Mike nodded in agreement, and I shuffled to the canoe, where Meathead sat patiently waiting for instructions. Sharkey waded more slowly than I had, laid his hands on either side of the dog's head, and dropped his own to rest upon it before inhaling deeply, breath verging on a wheeze. Then he lifted his head and placed a hand on my arm, rubbing it back and forth a few times.

"Protect Sydney," he said.

Sharkey stepped back and waved the dog toward the water. Meathead jumped in, without hesitation and more gracefully than I had, swimming behind me to the bank.

Mike followed as well, offering a hand as I stepped from the sucking mud to solid-ish land. It was an almost courtly gesture and, having fallen once already, one I gratefully accepted.

"Stay safe," he said.

"You too," I replied, too superstitious to say anything more.

A truck roared by above us, closer than the buffering north Florida jungle would have led me to believe was possible. I pulled my hat down tight, wary of wily branches, and picked my way toward the sound's source without looking back.

"Come on, Meathead. Now that's something I never thought I'd hear myself say," I muttered.

Thirty seconds a dog's master, and I was already narrating my life for his benefit. It was reassuring, having eighty pounds of fur and fangs walk alongside me. Falsely reassuring, though, I thought as I looked down at him. Cheerful as it was, his bright yellow life vest wouldn't protect either of us against a bullet.

14

The ragged shoulder of the two-lane highway was narrow enough to make me uneasy, as if I didn't have enough going in that department already. I hadn't thought to ask Sharkey for a leash. (*And where would he have been hiding said leash?* asked Snarky Me, while suggesting a few locations that are never meant for storage.) Fortunately Meathead walked easily behind me, single file, matching his pace to mine.

A single pickup passed us, heading in the opposite direction, before I saw the sign for Sharkey's driveway in the distance. You might think light traffic would relieve my anxiety (less chance of Meathead and I becoming roadkill), but that pernicious state was too well entrenched. Instead, I realized after the truck was gone that I should have flagged the person down and asked them to call for help. The single, lonely vehicle also reinforced my sense of isolation, which made me feel—you guessed it—uneasy.

To take my mind off my uneasiness, and the knowledge that it would be resolved *one way or another* very soon, I tried to get in character. During interviews, I often try to be the type of person I believe a witness will be most comfortable speaking with. But sometimes in the field I go a step further, assuming another identity in situations where to get what I want (and stay out of trouble), it's best to be someone other than Sydney Brennan, Private Investigator. It's like playing pretend for adults and getting paid for it. Outside of the bedroom.

Okay, I'm a chick with a dog. The guy waiting for Emmett might not have gotten a good look at Meathead, but he'd probably seen his yellow life jacket. It was hard to miss. I needed to stash it, and its extra cargo (meth? pot?) somewhere safe. I paused when we reached the *Sharkey's Canoe Shack* sign, its base and edges engulfed by Florida greenery even in February. Meathead sat next to me and waited patiently while my stiff, aching fingers (*God, my hands are a mess*) fumbled with his vest buckles. I nearly pulled the poor dog's head off when I missed a section of Velcro.

"Sorry, bud," I said, finally tugging the flotation device free.

I shoved the yellow-coated mass of Styrofoam (and drugs) in the tangled vegetation at the base of the sign, stepped back, adjusted some leaves, and then checked it again. Good enough. Now what? Okay, back to *chick with a dog*... That wasn't much to build on.

As I approached the parking lot, I pulled off my still-bloody shirt, wrung out the river water, and tied it around my waist. It was a tad chilly to go shirtless, but when entering an unpredictable situation, bikini boobs are always a good distraction. Alternatively, my fluorescent white torso would blind anyone not wearing protective glasses. While I was at it, I bent and shook out my half-wet, all-frizz hair and put my cap on backwards. My legs went loose-jointed as I sauntered into the parking lot like someone with a mellow dog, a philosophy, and half the earthly cares of Sydney Brennan, P.I. (Admittedly, half of my current cares would still be a lot.)

Among all the cars in the parking lot, Mike's yellow Jeep beckoned—with my cell phone—and I could have smacked myself for not getting the key from him. The outfitter's van that had taken us to the launch was back in its designated spot, and still trailer-less. I recognized two compact cars from this morning as well, presumably belonging to Leonard and Ken. But now there was a fifth vehicle, a mid-sized black SUV with a dented front bumper. Its tinted windows wouldn't hide the president (were he to slum it in a vehicle several years old), but they were dark enough that I couldn't be sure how many people sat inside. The driver's window was down, but a big man sat in the universal you-don't-see-me position, arm resting on the door and hand on his face, further blocking my view of the passenger's seat. On the plus side, he was so focused on the building and dock that he wasn't watching me.

Should I approach Driver Dude or the building first? I decided on the one I knew wasn't capable of carrying a weapon, striving for casual as I crossed the parking lot on a diagonal. The soles of my wet shoes made ticking sounds as they flung little bits of rock and sand through the air. I'd made it about halfway and was about to enter Driver Dude's field of vision when I saw something that stopped me in my tracks. There was another vehicle in the lot, one that didn't belong.

Sharkey's SUV, searched thoroughly and violently back at the launch, was now parked on the other side of the business van. How the hell had it gotten here? I wanted a better look, but then I might as well wave a sign at Driver Dude that read, "See me? Yes, I am also in this Up to My Eyeballs."

Motion within Driver Dude's vehicle made me wonder if he'd felt my attention. He dropped his arm, looking straight at me and Meathead, who'd paused when I did. I let out an audible sigh. There was only one thing for it.

Walking toward the clichéd but no less spooky black SUV, I wished I had a piece of gum to lubricate my dry mouth. I was getting too damned old for this shit. Double D rolled down his window when I reached the vehicle. He wore a baseball cap over his dark hair, and a long-sleeved navy button-down over a T-shirt with a sports logo I couldn't make out.

"Excuse me," I said, intending to lean on his car door to scope out the interior.

Driver Dude anticipated me, resting his own arm over the edge of the window as a barrier. I rolled with it, stretching my arms overhead to grip the top of the car, thankful I'd shaved my pits for the day's date. I saw no one else in the vehicle, though there was a large soda go-cup from a fast food restaurant in the passenger side cupholder and a crumpled bag from the same restaurant in the back.

"You lose a dog?" I asked.

"Did I what?" His voice had a similar cadence and twang as Emmett's, but was deeper, less whiny. Maybe because his head was less square.

"It's a pretty simple question," I said, dragging my own vowels a bit. "Did you lose a dog? This one was hanging out by the side of the road, decided to follow me. He's cute, and walks real good, but I've got cats."

He tilted his head to better see Meathead around his rearview mirror, and I tried not to flinch, conscious that I was wearing leggings and a bikini top and not much else. Meathead didn't react, except to test the air with his nostrils, which seemed to be his default state.

"No," he said. "That's not my dog." And he settled back in his seat, eyes forward as though I were no longer there.

"All right," I said, straightening. "I guess I'll go ask inside."

I'd only made it a few steps when he yelled, "Hey!"

I made a slow about-face, but kept my distance.

He looked around the parking lot ostentatiously and asked, "Where's your car? How'd you get here?"

Excellent question. Boyfriend? Little early in the day for that kind of drama. Hitchhiking? Even shirtless I wouldn't have made it far with no cars on the road. When in doubt, bore him to death...

"It's a long story. Last night my friend Julie says she wants to start exercising—" I gestured at my ridiculous pants, "—not that she needs to. I mean, it's good to be healthy, but she's not fat or anything. So we get up early, and she said since we were exercising, we should go by that donut place by the Super Walmart, 'cause they're real good and we'd just work it off. But then she remembered she had something to return, so we went in and by the entrance they had these plastic kayaks—super cheap! And so she said..."

Words kept coming out of my mouth, but he'd stopped listening. He pulled his arm back in the car and retreated behind his tinted windows.

My mouth fell open. "Jeez—rude much? I was trying to tell you I don't have a car and now Julie's not talking to me, so you could have at least offered me a ride."

Cinching my shirt more tightly around my waist, I stomped indignantly toward the gray building. Meathead followed me, as if he were the regular Sharkey's mascot. Maybe he was.

I stumbled at the front door (that push-pull thing always gets me), and once inside, the panic part of my brain screamed for me to run to the check-out counter, where I assumed they kept a phone. But I pushed the panic down, took a deep breath, and tried to slow my hammering heart.

I was safe for the moment. I hadn't seen a gun in Driver

Dude's vehicle. But then he wouldn't exactly leave it in the cupholder. The sweaty soda cup might tarnish its finish.

A figure passed by outside the large picture windows, carrying a cardboard box. Was that Ken? And if so, should I warn him about Driver Dude? The building must have a back exit, to deal with equipment issues without passing through the customer area. Ken had probably been back and forth all morning. I told myself that if Double D hadn't made his move yet, he wasn't going to just because Ken had stepped outside.

I walked past the kayaks for sale, finally reached the jutting corner that housed the back rooms, and peeked my head around the open space... there was no one else in the room. Now I ran toward the cashier's station. I rounded the massive counter on my way to the phone—

And found myself falling, feet caught on something. I grabbed for the counter as I toppled forward, but my hand slipped off its edge. There was nothing to break my descent.

Except the body on the floor.

"Ow!" it yelled.

I rolled off the not-a-corpse that lay beneath me, shaking my head to clear it. "Leonard, what the hell?" I asked the crushed teenager.

Meathead snuffled us, made sure we were both still breathing, and moved on out of the tight space.

Leonard rubbed his temple and tried to wriggle away from me, but there was nowhere to go. "I was fixing the internet cable. It gets loose under the—"

"You know what? I don't care. Listen, I know what you've been up to. Things got out of hand when Sharkey tried to fix it this morning, and he's in trouble. Mike and I found him on the river, and he's been stabbed."

"Oh, my God—stabbed?" Leonard's face blanched almost as sickly as his boss's.

Technically Sharkey had been sliced, not stabbed, but the verb was in the neighborhood and had gotten Leonard's attention. "The guy who did it is in the parking lot right now, waiting for Sharkey to show up. We have to call the police."

"But, but—" Leonard stammered, pushing his hair back from his face and picking at his lip. "We can't!"

"The hell we can't," I said, struggling to stand without kneeing the teen in the groin. I pulled myself up over the counter, and found myself face-to-face with his cousin Ken.

Leonard's gangly frame popped up next to me. "Ken," he said, voice breaking as though he'd just hit puberty. "I didn't hear you come in."

"I left the back door open because I was moving boxes," Ken said, dark brows lowering with suspicion. "What's going on, Leonard? And where's Sharkey?"

"I—I..." was as far as he got. The kid was developing a serious stuttering problem.

I shook my head and snatched at the phone on the desk, one of the big ones with multiple buttons and lines like I had in my own office. "Work out your family drama on your own time. Do y'all have nine-one-one service out here? And what do I need to dial to get an outside line?"

I must have been stressed, to lapse into a *y'all*. But Mike would be arriving any moment, with Emmett and Sharkey propped up in the canoe, and I dreaded hearing... anything, really. Any sounds from outside to indicate Driver Dude had seen them.

Ken put a finger over the hookswitch, while I still held the receiver midair. "Leonard," he asked, "where's the package?"

Well, shit.

I should have seen it coming. I would have, under normal circumstances, but *I wasn't supposed to have to think today.* In one, slow, shocked blink of an eye, it all came together. Of course. Who else would have driven Sharkey's SUV back here but Ken? He must have had a spare key and helped Emmett's friend move it, before someone else could stumble across it at the launch and call the cops.

"What package?" I asked. "Were you waiting for the Fed Ex guy? Because I didn't see him."

I pretended goosebumps engulfed my flesh because I was half naked and the air conditioning vent above my head had just sprung to life. It had nothing to do with preppy, polo-wearing Ken also wearing an expression so ominously calculating it belonged in a mob movie. His hand was as immobile as his face.

"Look, Ken, you missed the beginning of this," I riffed. "Somebody tried to steal Sharkey's SUV this morning at one of the boat launches. Mike and I found Sharkey downriver—in bad shape—and one of the guys who attacked him is out in the parking lot. I'm guessing he's waiting for his buddy to show up so they can rob your cash drawer. We need to call the police, before he shows up. I'm telling you, you really don't want to mess with these guys."

Ken seemed determined not to speak. I held the phone's receiver, and my tongue, wondering how long I should do either. Wondering when to stop pretending. I didn't see a weapon, but Ken was a big guy. There was another big guy—Driver Dude—waiting in the parking lot, likely armed, between me and the highway. The river was behind me (I'd spent enough of this February day swimming already), and I wasn't sure if anything lay between me and the exit door. Leonard stood so close his hip brushed against mine, and he was a wildcard.

The bigger man's attention was drawn to the windows behind me. "Well," Ken said, "it looks like we're too late."

There was movement by the docks, but with the canoe racks in the way, I couldn't make out the figures or even get a decent headcount. I moved around the end of the counter, still clutching the handset, trying to get a better view.

"Sydney, come with us to see who's arrived," Ken said, setting the phone's base on the counter.

"Thanks," I said, "but I'd really rather stay inside."

Ken nodded, smiling, but it was the kind of smile that meant nothing good. I started to back away, but his hand shot toward me so quickly I barely saw him move. He grabbed my wrist, squeezing it hard, and I gasped, almost dropping the handset.

"I'm afraid staying inside is not an option," he said.

Apparently Meathead felt otherwise. The dog was normally so silent, it was easy to forget he was there, as Ken must have done. A deep growl rumbled from his chest and throat, and his lips curled back in anticipation.

"Easy, Meathead," Ken said, releasing my arm and raising his own in supplication. "Easy, boy."

His eyes locked on the dog, and I seized my chance, swinging the handset backhanded at Ken's head as hard as I could. Before I'd finished that swing, I grabbed the phone's base in my right hand for a follow-up, also aimed at his head. And I kept swinging.

"You crazy fucking—"

Ken reached for me, hands catching my hair, and I screeched with pained anger. Meathead lunged for Ken's pants leg, snarling, and I heard snapping plastic as I got in a good lick with the phone, hard enough to make me drop it. Ken flailed, falling to his knees, then coiled into a ball to protect himself from Meathead. I kicked Ken—multiple times—aiming for his head so I wouldn't kick the dog. Or just because it was his head.

Ken seized at my leg, and I staggered sideways against the counter, scanning it frantically for another weapon. I gripped a ceramic mug by its handle, hauled back and—

"Stop!" Leonard said, grabbing my arm. Caught up in the moment, I nearly swung at the teen, but he backed away and begged, "Please stop."

I nodded, hands on my thighs, took a deep breath or five, and set the mug back on the counter.

"Is he dead?" Leonard asked.

I started to laugh, but the sight of Leonard's frightened face stopped me. "No," I said, looking down at Ken and huffing for breath. He was still curled tightly, but obviously conscious. "He probably won't even have a bruise tomorrow."

Slight exaggeration, but he was barely bleeding. Meathead had stopped his attacks when I stopped mine, and the dog sat, calm but alert, next to Ken's head. Which explained why Ken remained in a tuck. The man would need a new pair of jeans—the bottom of this pair was pretty well shredded.

Sort of like the landline.

"Dammit," I said, toeing bits of plastic and detached electronics with my sneaker. "Where's your cell phone?"

Leonard pulled it from his back pocket.

"Call the cops," I said. "Now."

Ken untucked his head long enough to shout, "No!"

I glared at him, and Meathead gave a slight rumble. "You really want to start that again? Because I think you've seen where the big dog stands on the issue."

"You don't understand," Ken pleaded.

"No—*you* don't understand!" I said, getting closer than was wise. "That asshole almost shot me. And Sharkey..."

My voice trailed off as I stepped back out of range and took a hard look at Mr. Preppy. Wondered what cruelties his innocent good looks had covered up over the years. "Or maybe you do understand. Maybe you understand completely. Leonard, call."

"What do I tell them?" he asked.

Not as stupid a question as it might seem. Even if he shared Preppy's genes, I was hesitant to throw poor Leonard under the bus. Sharkey obviously put a lot of stock in the young man. Of course, Sharkey had hired Ken, too. My mind raced.

"You don't have to give them details, especially about your involvement. Just say we have two, possibly three—" I glared at Ken, "—men who attacked your boss. We don't know if they're armed now, but they stabbed Sharkey and tried to shoot him, so we're going on the assumption they are. Give a description if you can. One of them has an injured knee. And make sure they send an ambulance for Sharkey."

Leonard nodded, gulping, and made the call.

"Guard this asshole," I told Meathead.

Unsure if that command was in the dog's vocabulary, I stayed close, straying only as far as the picture windows. My view of the far dock was still mostly blocked, but I could distinguish heads at multiple heights. Some standing and some still in the canoe? And what were the chances Emmett's partner was still in the parking lot?

Leonard approached me, off the phone now and giving his prone cousin and Meathead a wide berth.

"They're on their way?" I asked.

Leonard nodded.

"When?" I asked. He looked at me, blankly. "Leonard, what did they say about their ETA?"

He scratched at the back of his head and glanced nervously at his cousin on the floor. "Uh, I don't know. Soon?"

Soon. Soon is relative. *Soon* much of the state would be under water. *Soon* Glenn would fix the threshold at Cooper's. Neither of those timeframes would help Mike and Sharkey. They needed someone *now*.

I guess that made me someone.

"Leonard, you got anything in here to tie up Ken?" I asked.

For the first time, I saw a spark of something other than fear light up the teenager's face. "Oh yeah," he said. "I can definitely do that."

Ken started to speak, until I said (with a hand on Meathead's collar), "Shut it." Glancing over at the doors leading to the back, I told Leonard, "I want you to lock yourself in one of the back rooms with Ken, and don't open the door until a cop tells you to open it. No one else."

Leonard surprised me when he said, "No. I want to help Sharkey."

I shook my head. "Not happening. We need to keep you safe."

"I'm almost eighteen," he said, straightening his shoulders. "And it's my fault Sharkey's in trouble. Besides, how am I supposed to know if the person telling me to open up is a cop? The doors don't have windows."

The responsible, license-carrying Adult Sydney knew Leonard should be locked away where it was safe. But the part of me that came before her had been shut out of enough "adult" conversations and decisions (and rebelled enough in response) to make a pretty convincing argument that Leonard had a right to stay.

"Mouthy brat," I muttered.

"What?" Leonard asked.

"Not you," I said. "Okay, fine. But promise me if I tell you to run, you will. Promise me."

Leonard raised his hand in a gesture I assumed was related to the Boy Scouts. That, or he was raised by aliens. "I promise," he said, eyes wide and face serious.

Leonard brought out some kind of blue rope and tied Ken's hands behind his back while Meathead and I watched. Then we lifted Ken to his feet and led him to a room Leonard unlocked with a key that had been hidden beneath the cash register.

Mr. Preppy seemed to have lost some of his cockiness.

"I never meant for anything to happen to you or Sharkey," he said to his younger cousin. "I was just trying to help you out."

"I know," Leonard said.

I was glad Leonard did, because I knew—and certainly believed—nothing of the sort. "Sit on the floor," I said, gesturing for Leonard to bind Ken's feet as well.

The room was narrow, with heavy metal shelving along one wall. Most of the space was empty, except for scattered piles of office supplies. I picked up a roll of duct tape, my binding of choice because it required none of Mike's magic knot skills.

Ken sat at the edge of shelving, back against the wall and knees raised. "Leonard, why don't you just let me go? You know it'll kill my mom if I go to jail."

Leonard laughed as he cinched the rope tight around Ken's ankles. "No, Aunt Janine will kill *you* if you go to jail. Nice try, though."

Ken bucked forward, launching himself at Leonard. He made it to his knees, but overbalanced, tumbling onto his face. "You little cunt," he spat. "If your mother weren't such a no-good whore, we wouldn't have had to take care of you—"

I nudged Ken over with my foot, more gently than he deserved, temporarily cutting off his stream of vitriol. The sound of duct tape ripping from the roll competed with his grunting fall. I cut off the man's crap-spewing for good when I slapped a strip across his mouth. "I hope you forgot to shave this morning. Asshole."

Leonard's face was pale, whether because of Ken's words or the enormity of what he was about to do, I didn't know. I touched his arm gently. "Hey. You can still stay in here, you know. There's no shame in it."

He tucked his hair behind his ears and took a deep breath. "And stay locked in a room with that jerk? I don't think so."

He preceded me out of the room, gave Meathead a pat while he waited, then locked the door behind us. "Now what?"

I was still holding the roll of duct tape. I slid it up my arm like a bracelet and pointed to a door with raised eyebrows to ask, *outside?* Leonard nodded. "Now we go get some bad guys," I said.

"Wait!" Leonard pleaded, grabbing at my arm. "What are we going to say?"

My teeth flashed, but instead of reassuring Leonard, the teen seemed unnerved, dropping my arm and taking a step back.

"Don't worry," I told him. "We'll give them someone else to be afraid of."

Leonard and I slipped outside and hugged the wall of the building, using the canoe shack for cover. When we reached the picture windows, a superstitious impulse made me glance in the building, afraid there was someone watching us from within. There was no one, but the glass reflection was a reminder that Meathead quietly heeled alongside me.

We paused at the canoe shack, simple wood framing with a corrugated roof overhead and what looked like heavy chicken wire to enclose it. Inside, canoes rested on equally simple wooden racks, stacked in several sets of four. On the far side, a couple of racks held plastic kayaks stacked more closely together. I squatted, bringing me to Meathead's eye level, and Leonard followed my lead. Not quite lined up with a visual gap, I adjusted my stance, and my knee popped.

I flinched, both from the pain and the loud noise, and Leonard's head swung toward me in accusation. Shrugging, I rubbed my knee gently. No one could have heard me, a good ten yards away with all the ambient river noise. But my pulse still rippled into my throat as I gazed through the narrow space between the canoes.

I heard a murmur of speaking voices, but couldn't make out the words. A pair of jean-clad legs stood on the dock, presumably Driver Dude arrived from the SUV. Unless he regularly kept it holstered to his upper thigh (the only portion of him visible), I had no way of knowing whether Double D was showing a weapon. Sharkey's and Emmett's heads were in view, sitting in the canoe with Sharkey in front. Mike's neck and shoulders brought up the rear, his head "out of frame." I couldn't read Sharkey's or Emmett's expression from here.

"Are you ready?" I silently mouthed at Leonard.

He nodded, but his eyes were wide and his chest heaved for air, even while breathing through his nose. I patted his cheek, hoping to annoy or embarrass him enough to snap him out of his panic and stood, bracing myself for a popping knee that never happened. I interpreted the joint's behavior as a positive sign and strode from behind the canoe shack with (fake) confidence.

"Oh, good—you made it! I forgot to ask Ken about a patch kit for the other canoe. Will duct tape help?" I asked, holding my arm high so the tape scooted up to my elbow.

The man on the dock faced me. I thought he recognized me, but couldn't be sure. Driver Dude wasn't openly brandishing a gun, but he kept his right hand suspiciously close to his side. Pausing a couple of body lengths away, I nodded at Double D. "I didn't realize you guys knew each other."

Then I turned my attention back toward the canoe. Sharkey was barely upright in the bow, leaning to one side and gripping the wedge of the V-shaped nose. Emmett's posture was similar, and his hands were still bound. He hadn't spoken since I'd arrived. I figured that was somehow Mike's influence, his jaw tightly clenched in the stern.

"Emmett, how's the knee doing?" I asked.

"It hurts like a motherfucker," he said. "What do you think?"

"I think it's time Sharkey saw a doctor, and time you saw a vet. Mike, Leonard and I settled up with Ken, so we're good to go now," I said.

Emmett told Mike over his shoulder, "I think she's saying you can take the knife out of my back now, asshole."

That was one question answered, and one more thing I really didn't want to have to think about later. Mike held Emmett's knife in front of his chest and folded it closed before stowing it away again. I held my breath as Sharkey opened his mouth, hoping that he and Mike both had the sense not to follow up on my Ken bomb. A sound emerged, but nothing I could recognize as English, right before Sharkey's eyes rolled back in his head.

"Watch him!" I yelled, rushing toward the canoe. Leonard was faster, and didn't trip over Meathead as I did. The teen had the bow line in hand as Sharkey tumbled backward, landing on Emmett's leg. Leonard tugged the canoe snug against the dock and secured it while Emmett screamed and Meathead whined, a nasal, deeply unsettling ululation.

"What the hell is going on here? And where's the goddamn package?" Driver Dude demanded.

I kneeled next to the canoe, set the duct tape on the dock, and stretched an arm toward Emmett, who was senseless and still howling with pain. Turning to Double D, I said, "There's no way I can get him out of the canoe. I can help you once he's on the dock, but I can't reach him from here."

Glowering, Driver Dude pulled a gun from the small of his back, hidden beneath his shirt. And he pointed it at me. "The package," he repeated.

The dog's whine dropped to a low, rolling growl. "Easy, Meathead," I said, resting a hand on his side. "Stay."

"Dude, she told you, we gave it to Ken," Leonard said, voice shaking. "He said they told him it was okay, that we were good."

Now the man swung the gun toward Leonard. "*They* who?"

"I don't know, man." His voice betrayed him as it had this morning, jumping half an octave. "The guys he just called on the phone. I don't know who they are, but they're on their way over here. Can you point that somewhere else? Please?"

Emmett had settled down from constant vocalizing to a roar every few seconds, with a still-unconscious Sharkey lying on him.

"You know anything about this, Emmett?" the man asked.

Emmett shook his head, whether in pain or in answer was anyone's guess. He wailed, "Jesus, get him off me!"

"Shit," Driver Dude muttered, glancing over his shoulder at the parking lot, and then back toward the building. "You— get out of the canoe and haul him up here."

It wasn't hard to figure out he meant Mike, since Mike was the only person in the canoe both conscious and ambulatory. Mike stood carefully and stepped up onto the dock next to me. I probably couldn't have made it onto the dock without using the nearby swim ladder.

"I'm happy to see Emmett's backside, but I'll second what the kid said and ask you to point the gun elsewhere," Mike said. "Syd passed on the package, and we've got no beef with you."

"Fine. But toss the knife toward the parking lot," the man said, shoving his gun back beneath his shirt. "And I ain't taking this shit on faith. Leonard, bring Ken out here. I need to talk to him, *now*."

Leonard looked to me, but I couldn't say anything. All I could do was think, *stall for time, stall for time but DON'T bring him out here*, as loudly as possible and hope the kid was psychic. Or possessed a modicum of good sense.

"Okay, I'll get him," Leonard said, and ran down the dock toward the back door like a seven-year-old fetching a can of beer for his favorite uncle.

Mike watched him for a moment, then said, "Emmett, you need to pull yourself out from under Sharkey and sit up on the yoke. Can you do that?"

Emmett's bound hands flew to his face, pressing against his eye sockets. "I'm not feeling so good. Jesus. I think I'm gonna be sick."

Mike hunched over the edge of the dock, considering, then straightened and said, "Syd, give us a little room. And would you mind holding onto these for me? I don't want to lose them in the river."

He handed me his sunglasses, flinching momentarily as the sun assaulted his vision. Squinting, he struggled to stare at me significantly before his sun-dazzled eyes traveled over his shoulder toward Emmett's partner and back to me... Either Mike was about to have a seizure, or he was trying to tell me something.

"Got it," I said. At least, I hoped I did. "Are these the fancy glasses Richard made fun of you for buying?"

"Custom-fit is the word you're looking for," he said, feigning distraction as he kneeled on the dock and assessed the physics of retrieving the large gimpy man without drowning the unconscious one.

I untied my shirt from around my waist. "Okay, I'm wrapping your fancy glasses in my dirty shirt and setting them over here. Don't forget them."

Mike, torso now hanging over the dock, waved before threading his arms through Emmett's armpits and locking them. Mike groaned as he lifted the man, but his complaints were soon overpowered by Emmett's loud declarations of pain. Mike dragged Emmett slowly from beneath Sharkey, minimizing the likelihood of doing further injury to the unconscious man. And still, Meathead resumed his whining ululations.

I was wasting precious seconds watching. *Come on, Brennan, focus.* Meandering to the back of the dock, I left my shirt (and Mike's sunglasses) where the plank construction met the raised ground that ultimately became the parking lot. Then I crept toward Driver Dude, staring at his shirt where it hung over his jeans and his weapon. Was the gun centered? To the right of his spine? He'd held it right-handed earlier. I extended my hand toward him, as though trying to grab a creature I wasn't sure I wanted to touch but knew I needed to get rid of. Could it be this easy?

Of course not.

Gravel crunched as a vehicle entered the parking lot—still out of sight from water level, but we all heard it, heads swiveling. I tried to look innocent as Driver Dude took in our new proximity. Before he could comment on our coziness, the back door of the business banged open, and Leonard came running around the canoe shack and into view.

"Sorry!" he panted. "Ken said he'll be here in a minute, but he had to go meet those guys first."

Driver Dude's eyes darted from Leonard to the parking lot, and I knew he was going for his gun again. Sounds and movements and thoughts simultaneously slowed down and jumbled together. Having nearly hauled Emmett onto the dock, Mike suddenly dropped him back into the canoe. The vessel capsized with the impact, sending Emmett and Sharkey overboard. Emmett was thumping and screaming, Leonard was yelling, Meathead was snarling, and everything was in motion. Leonard ran to the river, there was splashing everywhere, all while Mike and I lunged at Driver Dude—and his gun—from opposite sides.

I was closer, but not close enough. I watched Double D, in one motion, pull the gun free from his back and pivot toward the parking lot. And me. I dropped low and slammed a foot into his leading knee, as I'd wanted to do to Emmett hours ago. It wasn't a square kick, but the impact knocked both of us down and he lost the gun.

It skidded across the dock and I scrambled after it, planks hard beneath my knees, registering in my peripheral vision that Driver Dude was nearly upon me. But there it was. A gun on the ground. *Again*. Except this time, unlike three months ago, I wasn't fumbling in the dark.

All metal and textured plastic, the firearm fit awkwardly in my too-small hand. Then in both hands, after I pushed myself to standing. *Red dot*—it did have a safety, and it was off. I kept the handgun pointed low as I spun, expecting two hundred pounds of pissed-off Driver Dude to knock me down at any moment.

But he had his hands full, too.

Mike and Driver Dude sprawled on the dock, semi-upright, both facing me. Mike was pinned against Double D's chest by one thick arm, between Double D's raised knees. Double D's other arm held a knife to the base of Mike's throat. Not Sharkey's pocketknife, or even Emmett's folding one, but a wicked knife with a few inches of serrated, fixed blade fit to gut an alligator. I could see the sheath on his belt now that his shirt was out of the way and I was looking for it.

"Give me the gun," Driver Dude said, not as winded as I would have liked.

"Fuck you," I replied, praying that all of my considerable shaking was still only on the inside. *Get in character, Syd. Be someone else. Someone who isn't afraid to pull the trigger. Again.*

"Okay, here's what's gonna happen," Driver Dude said. "You'll leave the gun on that deck post, right next to where you left your boyfriend's sunglasses. I'll let your boyfriend go, and then the gun leaves with me."

"What about Emmett?" I asked. The upside-down canoe was a dark shape in my periphery, but I didn't dare take my eyes from Driver Dude.

"Survival of the fittest," he said.

My gaze, alternating between his face and the blade at Mike's neck, strayed to the area in between. To Mike's face. He was short of breath, too, his cheeks slightly flushed, eyes focused somewhere above my head, expression unreadable... Maybe that was the point. Maybe that's what Mike was trying to give me.

"Sorry, you don't get the gun," I said. "But if you leave now —without Mike—I won't shoot you."

Driver Dude had lost his hat, his dark hair plastered to his narrow skull from pressure and sweat. But he hadn't lost his temper. Would he really slit Mike's throat? Slice across the jugular and carotid and bathe himself in Mike's blood? Or maybe it didn't actually work that way. And maybe Double D already knew that.

"I'd say that gun's a little heavier than this knife," he said. "Of course, I get to rest my arm on your boyfriend's nice big chest, too."

I didn't have anything to say. I also didn't have a shot. Even if I'd had no qualms about shooting a man in the head, it was beyond my skill to do so with a gun I'd never shot before. At least, not without a good chance Mike would be the man with a bullet in his brain. The same went for any maiming target, like Driver Dude's pointed knees. Not to mention a good, solid shot could still have a funky ricochet, or pass completely through him.

"Just out of curiosity, you ever shot a gun before?" Driver Dude asked. Mike hissed involuntarily as the knife tip pressed into his long, pale throat and blood trickled onto his shirt near his left shoulder. "You ever shot a man before?"

Whatever you do, Brennan, don't flinch.

I pointed at the shallow embankment to their left, feet braced and leaning slightly forward, and slowly pulled the trigger. I felt the recoil roll into my shoulder and even my jaw. There was a small kick of soil, but nothing like you'd see on TV.

"The gun seemed to work, so I guess I have the first part down," I said, finger still on the trigger. "You want to take a chance on being my second?"

Thoughts rebounded in my skull, *Please don't call my bluff* fighting against *I'll blow your goddamn head off.*

We stared at each other, the gun getting heavier with every passing second. Had he planted that seed, or would I be feeling its weight no matter what? I heard a roaring in my ears—*shit, don't go passing out, Brennan.*

Then Meathead barked, a deep, echoing sound from the direction of the river, and the roaring resolved into distinct sounds: vehicles again—the engines of multiple vehicles, and gravel, and footsteps...

"Get down! Weapons on the ground and hands behind your head!" boomed a voice. Or maybe voices.

I hesitated, eyes on the man with the knife. Waiting.

"I said, weapons on the ground—now!"

The cavalry was here; men and at least one woman in uniform and wearing protective gear swirled around the property. I raised my hands like a cactus, then squatted slowly and placed the gun on the dock. I didn't bother with the safety, afraid I'd pull the trigger attempting to slide the button one-handed.

I watched as Driver Dude dropped his knife. Mike sat up, hands behind his head, while a cop rolled Driver Dude over and searched him.

Then a man's voice ordered, firmly but not too loud since he stood close to me, "On your knees."

He could have saved his breath.

My legs buckled with relief, spilling me onto the dock. No thought necessary.

I hadn't spoken to Mike yet, or anyone else not in uniform, with the exception of Sharkey. There had been some miscommunication about my relationship with the injured man (which I didn't bother to correct), and they gave us a moment together before the ambulance took him away. He was conscious, but in a lot of pain.

"Don't worry," he said, "I won't charge you for the damage to my canoe."

I geared up to yell at him, until I realized he was joking. Feeling magnanimous, I replied, "Then Mike and I won't sue for pain and suffering."

He opened his eyes wide and stretched his forehead, as though fighting sleep. "About Leonard..."

"I'll take care of it," I said. "I actually have a meeting tomorrow morning with the attorney I mentioned. I think I can talk him into representing Leonard."

He nodded. "Good. You know, he saved my life."

"So I gathered."

Apparently both Leonard and Meathead jumped in the river when the canoe capsized, and between them, had kept

Sharkey afloat until help arrived. No one had bothered about Emmett, but he was taken into custody after he was found clinging to the dock's swim ladder.

I rose to leave, but Sharkey gripped my hand with one that already sported an IV. "Wait, Sydney. If anything today... scared you—"

A single chuckle escaped me.

"I mean, about Mike. Or, I don't know—*bothered* you... please come back sometime. We'll camp out, relax." Sharkey smiled. It was the first time I'd seen the expression on the man, and it suited him. "I'll send Mike to get firewood, and then I can answer all your burning questions about our Mr. Montgomery. But please don't hold this against him."

I was so wrung out, for a moment I thought I'd cry. "Don't worry," I managed. "I won't."

After leaving Sharkey, I escorted a couple of officers—or rather, they escorted me—to the roadside sign to retrieve his clandestine handiwork. A short, dark-haired woman grunted in appreciation as she examined Meathead's life jacket with gloved hands. "Nifty," she said.

"I thought so," I admitted. "He said it's just —"

There was a tearing sound as the officer figured it out on her own. She peeled back the fabric just far enough to expose the edge of a light brown rectangle heavily taped and wrapped in clear plastic.

"What is it?" I asked.

"That's a call for the lab guys," she said. As if she couldn't make an educated guess.

Fine, be that way.

With the important bits out of the way, she and her colleague returned me to the controlled chaos that had engulfed Sharkey's Canoe Shack. I was passed around a bit more, occasionally questioned, until an EMT—another woman—cleaned the wound on my neck.

My hand brushed the fresh bandage at my throat. "I'm already pretty pale," I said.

"So I see," she said, staring pointedly at my bare torso.

They'd kept my bloody shirt, and I was still only wearing my bikini. "So I guess if I start to crave human blood..."

"I wouldn't worry about that, but keep an eye on it," she said, snapping off a glove. "Be a shame if they had to amputate."

I started to shiver, and she handed me a scratchy blanket. "That was a joke."

"I'm hoping my sense of humor returns with my red blood cells," I said, feeling suddenly overwhelmed by the requirements of interacting with other humans. I couldn't seem to stop touching the bandage, tentatively, as though the wound would bite. "What do you think the chances are of me camping out in the bathroom for a while? Alone?"

"Wait here," she said.

I leaned against a vehicle, but wasn't there long before she returned and motioned me to follow. A few officers milled around inside the business—I assumed someone had rescued Ken from the storeroom, although I hadn't seen him—but the ladies' room was empty.

"They're wrapping up, so have it," she said.

I thanked her, and when she'd left I made my way to the smaller of the two stalls. Unlike most public restrooms, this toilet actually had a lid and looked as though it had been cleaned sometime this calendar year. Grateful, I sat on top in my skuzzy pants, pulled my feet up after me and wrapped the blanket around the tight ball I had become. I even pulled the blanket over my head and closed my eyes.

It had been a long day. I was exhausted, physically and emotionally, so much so that I didn't really care what we'd been caught in the middle of. Maybe that would change after a decent meal and a good night's sleep. But for now there was just one thing my over-stimulated, overwhelmed brain could not let go... had I confessed to murder?

You ever shot a gun before? Driver Dude had asked. And then, *You ever shot a man before?* I'd fired wide into the bank, noted the gun worked. Then I'd intended to answer the latter question, *You want to take a chance on the second?* But somehow my unconscious had gone all Freud on me and interjected something else. Or so I suspected. I wasn't sure exactly what I'd said, and certainly not what Mike had heard. Did it matter? Surely Mike would chalk it up to me misspeaking under duress.

Except Mike was the only person who knew anything about what Glenn and I had done back in November. (The only person except Ralph, who wasn't the most reliable or disinterested witness under the circumstances.) Just the broadest outline—I'd kept the details from Mike to protect him. He'd said he understood and hadn't pushed, but I couldn't help believing the wall of knowing and not-knowing stood between us. When Mike wouldn't go with me on a surveillance job a couple of weeks ago, a tiny, dispirited part of me suspected that was why, that we couldn't get past the things we couldn't talk about. But then Mike had shown up after all (unexpectedly and with impeccable timing), followed by inviting me on our first real date. Had my Freudian slip brought the subject back into play?

Even if it hadn't, today's shared hazardous escapade was bound to bring any issues between us to the surface. Especially the fact that we'd tortured a man together. My stomach churned and bile gathered in the back of my throat. Yeah, that's the one I really didn't want to think about.

A knock at the bathroom door saved me from doing so. I unwrapped my blanket cocoon and roused myself, preparing to be interrogated. Or more likely, ignored while waiting to be interrogated. Again.

I opened the door to find Mike leaning against the wall, a couple of reusable grocery bags in hand. Imitating his insouciance, I leaned against the doorframe and propped the bathroom door open with my foot.

"You okay?" he asked.

"You seem to be asking me that question a lot today," I said. He ducked his head. Of course, it still hung several inches above me.

I tried to salvage the moment by adding, "Hey—I didn't mean... I don't know what I meant. Or what you think I meant. Look, let's not be dysfunctional."

As I had been, spinning out hypotheticals on the toilet, waiting for this moment.

It went against my nature to make the first move in a relationship. Well, the first *emotional* move, anyway. But, scary as the prospect may be, it was time to be a grown-up. The bathroom door thumped my butt as I limboed my face under Mike's *(I'd kiss him if I weren't afraid of breaking my neck)* and said softly, "No dysfunction. Okay?"

He smiled, said "Okay," and a hand drifted toward my face before returning to grip the bags. He held one up and said, "I thought you might want these."

I peeked inside and almost did a little dance—clean, dry clothes. "Thank you."

"You're quite welcome."

But I didn't remember packing a pair of navy blue sweatpants. I pulled them free far enough to sling one leg over my shoulder, exposing a pair of red boxer shorts as well. Smiling, I said, "I think you gave me the wrong bag."

Mike lifted the pants leg from my shoulder—it would've reached from my toes to approximately my chest—and said, "I believe you're right."

We switched bags and he saluted before heading to the men's room to change.

I felt almost like a new woman when I emerged from the restroom a few minutes later in my own gray sweats. A ravenous new woman.

Mike had tweaked the layout in the showroom. He sat in a camp chair, one of a pair arranged in front of the display canoe and kayaks with a collapsible table between them. He stood and waved me to the other chair, scooting it in for me as though we were in a restaurant. Two bottles of cold soda rested on the table.

"Fine wine to accompany our meal?" I asked.

"Courtesy of Levi's cooler. He left me the keys to lock up, and I figured it was the least he could do. I'm afraid our food didn't survive. But at least it was the only casualty."

Reaching for a soda, my arm paused midair. My chest constricted, and my hand shook. I could feel Mike's eyes on me, but stared at the accordion-like plastic tabletop as I tucked my hand under my hip and cleared my throat. "Sorry. I think my blood sugar bottomed out."

He cracked my soda open and set the bottle on the table, cap next to it, before opening his own. I chugged until the fizzing burned my nose and made my eyes water, and mostly avoided baptizing my dry shirt with sticky, sugar water. Shaking my head to clear it, I said, "That's a good year."

"I thought so," he agreed. His hands fidgeted with his soda cap, rotating it one direction, then the other. "You know, Syd, what happened today... it wasn't *about us*. It had nothing to do with us."

"As individuals, or as an 'us'?" I asked.

"Either one," he said. "We just fell into it. We like to think things happen because we set events in motion in our lives. But more often than not, people fall into things."

"I agree that sometimes shit just happens," I admitted, taking a more modest sip as the sugar and caffeine started to kick in. "But what about when we fall into a situation, and it gets worse simply because we're in it? What if the ripples we make when we fall in trigger a tsunami? A shit tsunami?"

The corner of his mouth twitched. "Aside from the bad science—"

"We're talking philosophy, not science," I said, the corner of my own mouth twitching.

"Then I think that philosophy both overestimates your— that is, *our*—importance to the world—"

I felt blood and indignation rush through my body.

"And underestimates your propensity for doing good. For helping people." He blushed. "For making the world a better place, just by being in it."

My eyes filled; I was speechless.

A sudden knock at the door startled us both. My body went still except for a single hard blink, while Mike's jaw clenched, and his squeezing fingers mauled his bottle cap. In the next instant, his face cleared and he smiled. "I'll be right back."

I waited until he passed to quickly wipe away tears that had spilled down my cheeks. Eyes still blurry, I heard him speaking with someone. Then the door closed, and I was nearly overcome by an incredible, delectable scent.

Mike set the flat box on the camp table in front of me—it barely fit—and yet I still couldn't believe my senses. "Pizza?" I asked.

A full-fledged Montgomery grin crept across his face, and his left cheek stuck at half-mast as he spoke. "Mushroom and olive. It'll be dark soon, and I know you have to leave, but you can't drive hungry. One of the deputies was a softy. When I told him this was supposed to be our first date, he gave me a number and said to use his name if they balked at delivering."

He flipped the lid open and I inhaled deeply, almost amorously. "Mmm-hmm, this is the kind of law enforcement corruption we can all get behind. Mike Montgomery, you are definitely a keeper."

"You think?" he asked, voice surprisingly tentative.

His hesitancy evoked such a feeling of tenderness—*I must really be exhausted*—that I gripped the seat beneath me to keep from tearing up again. My fingernail scratched its fabric, explored its texture until I was sure my voice wouldn't falter. "Processing the past eight hours—what we did, what was almost done to us—that'll take time. But that's okay. We've got time."

We leaned in—I'm not sure which of us was first—and our warm, chapped lips met. Mike's hand gently gripped the back of my head, working his fingers into my damp hair. The longer his mouth lingered on mine, the more grateful I was for the support. I finally pulled back with a heavy sigh, light-headed enough to grip the table.

"But maybe we should do something..." I found myself smiling as I finished, "More traditional for our second date."

He grinned.

"You think?" he asked again, but this time with confidence. Confidence, and, as he led my lips back toward his, a little tongue. I found myself tingling in all the places a girl likes to tingle.

Still, when we came up for air, I couldn't leave it there. "I know we have a lot to talk about later—not now—and I said we wouldn't be dysfunctional. But I do have one question..."

"I was just about to elbow that guy in the gonads," Mike said.

And then bleed out all over him, I thought but kept to myself. After all, *his* attacker hadn't been semi-conscious. I figured Mike was joking, but I couldn't be sure. "No, my question is about your former spouse. You really do have an ex-wife?"

"Yes," Mike moaned. "Of all the things you could have forgotten while in fear for your life—"

"Just one question about the woman who legally shared your bed."

"Where is it illegal—"

"Shh!" I said, touching his lips, then pinching them gently between my fingers. They were already pink. "Stop distracting me."

My throat flushed with heat, and I reminded myself I was heading home soon, that I had to leave and we were taking it slow. *That's right, Brennan, slow—bring it down a notch before you do something you won't regret at all.*

"Okay, what's the one question?" Mike asked, voice husky.

I moved closer, resting my arm on his, my breath brushing his ear as I stared at a single gray hair in his sideburn. Maybe it was blonde. I almost teased it out to check—I really am easily distracted. Or I was just thrilled at long last to have "permission" to be distracted by the individual hairs on his head. By the smell of his shampoo (no idea—it was lost beneath river reek; I'd have to check another day). By the closeness of him and the promise that he'd be this close again. Finally, I spoke in Mike's ear, voice scarcely above a whisper, "This ex-wife of yours... could I kick her ass?"

His breath caught, then he threw his head back and laughed, a deep, hearty laugh without subtext, the kind brought forth when a man knows all will be right with the world. In a quick, un-Mike-like motion, his long arms swept me up and lifted me onto his lap. (Yep, his back would definitely be feeling it tomorrow.) I squeaked and prayed the camp chair would hold us both, but his body still shook beneath me with laughter.

Mike squeezed me to his chest, cheek against my hair, and said, "Sydney, I'd put my money on you any day of the week."

ABOUT THE AUTHOR

A recovering criminal attorney, Judy K. Walker has enough spare letters after her name (and student loan debt) to suggest insatiable curiosity is something fictional private investigator Sydney Brennan inherited from her creator. Fortunately, Judy's curiosity rarely involves murders. She also writes the *Dead Hollow Trilogy*, an Appalachian thriller series with a touch of the paranormal that taps into her West Virginia origins. Judy writes from her home in Hawaii, where she is surrounded by husband, dogs, cat, and assorted geckos. If she's not tapping away at her computer, she's probably sweeping tumblepuppies (piles of accumulated critter hair).

Many readers need an extra nudge to take a chance on an Indie Author, because—let's face it—they're afraid one of my dogs barfed on the keyboard and I hit "Publish." If you enjoyed *River Bound*, please consider leaving a quick review on your retailer or book review site of choice—just a few lines will do. Thank you!

Learn more about Sydney Brennan's world and connect with me online at:
www.judykwalker.com